About the Author

She had always been an avid reader, tracing her passion back to the moment she was handed her first take-home books at the age of four: *Peter and Jane*. That love for reading had persisted throughout her life, blossoming into a newfound passion for writing. With a loving husband, Wade, by her side, along with their two children, she found herself deeply immersed in the joys of family life. Their home is nestled in Perth, Western Australia; a place where their shared moments created the tapestry of their lives. Her family is not just her world; they are her everything.

This is the first book of a series.

Needing

Justine Robertson

Needing

Vanguard Press

VANGUARD PAPERBACK

© Copyright 2024
Justine Robertson

The right of Justine Robertson to be identified as author of
this work has been asserted by her in accordance with the
Copyright, Designs and Patents Act 1988.

All Rights Reserved

No reproduction, copy or transmission of this publication
may be made without written permission.
No paragraph of this publication may be reproduced,
copied or transmitted save with the written permission of the publisher, or in
accordance with the provisions
of the Copyright Act 1956 (as amended).

Any person who commits any unauthorised act in relation to this publication
may be liable to criminal prosecution and civil claims for damages.

A CIP catalogue record for this title is available from the British Library.

ISBN 978-1-83794-390-6

This is a work of fiction. Names, characters, businesses, places, events and
incidents are either the products of the author's imagination or used in a
fictitious manner. Any resemblance to actual persons, living or dead, or actual
events is purely coincidental.

*Vanguard Press is an imprint of
Pegasus Elliot Mackenzie Publishers Ltd.*
www.pegasuspublishers.com

First Published in 2024

**Vanguard Press
Sheraton House Castle Park
Cambridge England**

Printed & Bound in Great Britain

Dedication

For my family.

Acknowledgements

Thank you to my family, friends and colleagues who took the time to read through every version of this book I wrote and for their constant support. Thank you to my son, who, whenever I wasn't writing, brought my book and pen to me in the hopes of a bigger inheritance.

Chapter 1

I know what you are. I know what you've done. This needs to stop now.

Alice looked down at the slither of non-descript paper that had been pushed under her hotel room door. It hadn't been there when she went to bed, and she hadn't heard anything in the hallway outside the door. Standing on her tiptoes, she looked through the peephole. All clear, nothing, no one out there. Well, that's strange. She hardly knew anyone well enough for such a bizarre note to be left. Alice couldn't help but smile. No one knew the real her, no one. She had made sure of that. It had never crossed her mind that she would ever be found out or that she would ever be on anyone's radar. She was not that careless. Or was she just too cocky for her own good?

What in the world? she thought.

'What was she? What had she done?'

To anyone else, it may have been obvious. Not Alice. She only saw herself as a hardworking, upstanding member of society. She was always helping others and was always ready to right wrongs, not letting anyone get the better of her.

The note, however, made her a tad nervous. Who was this person, and what did they know? It was pretty creepy to think someone was watching her. She was the one always watching. That was her thing. Alice had spent her life making sure she wasn't seen, and now this. What had she missed? *Interesting,* Alice thought. *Very interesting.* She would need to start being more aware of her surroundings.

Scooping up the paper, Alice tucked it into her purse. A mystery that would have to wait. She had plans for the day, and nothing was going to get in the way of them. Grabbing her handbag, she headed out. A day in Freo was just what she needed.

The middle of summer in Fremantle (Freo to the locals) saw people from all walks of life flock to the many cafés, bars and restaurants. An amazing place to relax and unwind. Catching people off guard was easy in such an environment. Just what she was looking for. Fremantle has become the epicentre for families and tourists, with cruise ships and navy fleets docking in port. Making for a vibrant multicultural hub. Trains running every fifteen minutes from the city meant there was always a steady stream of visitors wanting to explore. One hundred and ninety-four years of history boasting Victorian architecture that provides remnants of Australia's days as a British Penal colony drew in the crowds. The perfect place for anyone looking to people watch. White sandy beaches to the west meet the expanse of the Swan River to the east, flowing directly to the heart of Perth City. The contrast between the coastal town and the bustling business centre of Perth where she stayed between shifts was worlds apart. It was easy to forget the time in Fremantle; with its laid back vibe, unlike the workers in the city that found themselves counting the hours until the end of their day, releasing them from the mundane life of the nine-to-five. Alice needed to forget the world for a while and Freo was just the place for that.

In a quiet corner on the café strip, Alice sat watching a small group of young tourists, as they excitedly discussed their plans for the day. Alice's excitement was something else. Simmering below the surface she could feel the heat rising, slowly creeping in from the darkest part of her thoughts. The watching and waiting always got her heart racing, but this was something new. She must bide her time. She must wait and watch, blending in unnoticed. She needed to work out why she was feeling these things, while being careful to avoid any contact or make herself recognisable. That was the beauty of everyday workout gear and a low-sitting peak cap. It hid her slender frame and dark, striking features perfectly. She looked just like any other gym goer after early morning classes. Although the gym wasn't her favourite form of exercise, she loved a good run, it helped keep her trim figure in check and clear her mind of intrusive thoughts. Years of practice had allowed Alice to blend into the background with ease.

'There's no rush, there's no rush,' she told herself. Alice tried to slow her breathing and her heart rate. It had been a while since she had allowed her dark thoughts to be in charge, and she could feel her blood pressure rising.

'Can I get you something, another drink perhaps?' asked an overly friendly waitress.

Great, Alice thought. *This is precisely what I was trying to avoid.*

'Just another of the same, please,' Alice spoke quickly, trying to avoid being rude and making a scene, but wanting to get her to move on as quickly as possible. She didn't need or want the attention.

She could hear the young tourists talking candidly. Two girls in their twenties and a male possibly a bit older, the hint of a German accent could be heard. Alice did love listening to the accents of Europeans; young, naive travellers who had been away from their homes for years, going from one job to the next all around Australia, lugging their backpacks as they went. Huge gaps in not speaking to friends and family back home. Making them unwittingly easy targets for mishaps. Australia provided the safe escape, at face value, that these young adults were looking for, but below the surface there had always been the underlying threat of something far more sinister. An abundance of work opportunities in every state provided the cash they needed to continue their travels, whether in a camper van just purchased on arrival or the many buses and trains running between cities.

They were also known to hitchhike occasionally, although some had been put off by the tales of Ivan Milat in NSW, a notorious serial killer who preyed on the innocence of backpackers. Hollywood didn't help either, igniting fears that hadn't existed until the release of *Wolf Creek*, which saw the end of that style of travel for most through WA. However, time passes, and people relax again and forget what really needs to be remembered.

A week earlier, Alice had sat in a café not far from the one she found herself in today. After her red-eye flight from Melbourne, she'd ventured into Fremantle to enjoy the people-watching. She had never expected to be drawn to someone in this way. This was more like stalking. Alice had never been one to stalk. She had never gone out of her way to watch someone. The pull towards this group was something very strange and intense. With the far more relaxing atmosphere in Freo, it was easy for her to take her time and watch from afar. No one would suspect they were being watched. This time of year was for soaking up the sun, having drinks and catching up for laughs. They would never imagine that a stranger was lurking just near taking in every bit of their conversation.

It was in that café, she had first heard the group of Germans talking loudly about their upcoming travel plans. They would stay in Fremantle for a few more months, but the male of the group would be leaving in eight days to venture up north to Broome with the promise of new work. Which meant Alice would only have a short time frame to make this work.

Taking out her phone, Alice checked her work roster and knew she would be back in Perth in six days, leaving her two days before her next flight out. Those two days would be plenty of time to execute her plan and slip back out of the state unnoticed. Being a flight attendant had its perks, travelling from state to state, coming and going with ease, no questions asked.

So here she was six days later. Catching the train from her city hotel, it hadn't taken her long to walk down the café strip and find the group. Even though Fremantle was full of tourists and working backpackers, these three stood out. The girls with hair white as snow and the male a good five inches taller than them with dark, striking features. Alice had since found out, from her eavesdropping, that his name was Otto.

Otto had caught her eye last week, not overly muscular or much taller than Alice. She knew if it came to it, he wouldn't be much of a challenge physically. At 5'6", she was strong. Although she wouldn't call herself a gym junky, she knew it was a necessity. If she was going to do this she needed to make sure she was physically ready for whatever came. Most of all, she knew she could outsmart anyone. Her brains rather than brawn were her greatest asset by far. Alice did not know what it was about Otto that drew her to him. It wasn't like the other times the burning had started. They had been opportunistic encounters rather than this throb of yearning she was experiencing This was a low burning, just simmering below the surface, making her need to find out more. She had not had first-hand contact with Otto; he had not spoken to her, and she had not spoken to him. This was new to Alice. When the burning started, her previous encounters had been those that had wronged her, those that had taken from her. Otto was nothing like what she had encountered before. She had no idea what was pulling her to him.

She had learnt over the years and from past encounters, that were extremely impulsive, that her planning needed some work. Everything needed to be planned to the very second, or mistakes were made, and then you were finished. She'd watched enough documentaries over the years to know that a tiny slip-up made everything come crashing down. Being a woman meant Alice had other challenges her male serial killer counterparts did not have to worry about. Dragging a dead weight was not ideal, even with her fitness training, avoiding this would come down to thorough planning.

As she sat there, Alice plotted, plotted her every move down to the last second of what she would need to do over the next day and a half before her flight. She knew it wouldn't be hard to get Otto alone. The group were planning one last hoorah tomorrow night, and Alice knew exactly where they would be. Drunk people made for easy prey. Their guards would be down more than ever, never suspecting what was to come.

After listening for a bit longer, Alice slowly stood to pay, making sure her back was to the German group.

'Have a lovely day,' smiled the waitress who had served Alice earlier.

'Thanks.'

It would be lovely, Alice thought but not for any of the reasons the waitress was thinking; she had lots to do before tonight.

Chapter 2

Alice's fascination for all things dark didn't start with killing family pets or collecting roadkill like well-known serial killers now immortalised on TV and in movies. Still, she knew from a very early age what she was to become.

Reflecting on those early years, Alice remembered how her thoughts always seemed to verge on the macabre, thoughts that didn't allow Alice the perfect childhood like the kids around her. She rarely saw the good in her life. Watching from afar, learning the art of knowing people's thoughts and feelings instantly had become a game changer for Alice. Lying and manipulation would become second nature to her, mastering both at a very early age. There was no one she couldn't read like a book and no one she couldn't manipulate.

Easily able to pick that one lost soul in a crowd of people, being drawn to their aching and loneliness, their yearning for companionship or just that average obnoxious tosser at the bar that the world was better off without. Yes, Alice knew instantly who was right for this world and who was not. She prided herself on it.

Those that the world was better off without. People who took it upon themselves to inflict hurt and suffering on others. These were the type of people Alice avoided the most. When they couldn't be avoided, she would act.

As Alice got older, it was easier and easier to see the things she disliked in people, but acting on it was another thing altogether. She had no time for annoying people, all her patience was depleted, she didn't need to worry any more about what anyone thought of her, and she didn't care about trying to make everyone happy. She had wasted so much of her childhood trying to keep them happy that she had lost all sense of herself at times. No emotions came easy for Alice. It was pretending that she had them that was hard for her. She had learnt early to hide her lack of feelings from those closest to her. Her mother was forever watching, trying to catch her off guard and watching how she reacted to every situation. When Alice didn't act like her mother expected her to, there were threats of doctor visits and fights with her father about how she was weird. So nice of a mother to think such things about their child.

Her need for attachment had been far more complex to just turn off. Not always liking people, or knowing how to act in social situations, was hard for Alice to form any type of attachment, but when she eventually did, it was intense. The need for attachment was the driving force that would see Alice become who she was today – needing to be needed, wanting to be wanted. Even those without emotion need someone they can rely on, someone who relies on them. It was human nature.

However you look at it, it's what Alice longed for, and not having it became the start of why her future was playing out the way it was now.

Alice Munroe was five or six when she realised she wasn't really like her cousins or the other kids around her. She was an only child, making it easier for her mother to compare her to others. Her parents had decided not to have more children after Alice. Her mother had stated to anyone and everyone, in front of Alice, that would listen, that Alice was more than enough to worry about. Of course, to her being different was a good thing. Alice knew early on she was smarter than the other kids. Toys didn't interest her. The disgust Alice felt watching other kids play with dolls or dress-ups made her want to throw up. It was a physical reaction to a very normal situation, but the idea of play was totally lost on Alice. She had never been around kids long enough to even learn to mimic their idea of play. She considered it a waste of time, preferring her books over human conversation. The joy of play doesn't exist when you have no feelings or imagination. Her thoughts often not allowing her to see the light in everyday things. They always drew her back to the safety of the dark. Where her thoughts were her thoughts, hers alone. She never relaxed enough to be open to anything other than the dark thoughts, never wanting others to know what she was thinking. This infuriated her mother. Her mother could not get a read on her and it seemed to Alice that she never made the effort to even try and understand her, not knowing is what frightened her mother.

To Alice, she was perfectly normal. To Alice, everyone else was the problem. Blending into her surroundings became how she survived. No one noticed when she didn't join in or when other kids gave her a wide berth, except maybe her mother. They say kids are very intuitive. They knew to stay clear of her.

She was happy to oblige, watching from afar, learning their every mannerism. She picked up on certain traits, memorising them and ensuring she knew all about a person's body language. Staying quiet was her way of keeping her dark thoughts loud and her emotions dead.

School was just another stepping stone for her. Her head was constantly buried in books, her happy place, knowing it was her best chance to escape the suburbs of Perth. Alice knew there was more for her out in the world, and it wouldn't be long before she started planning her escape. It had become harder and harder to just blend into the background as she grew. She needed more than Perth had to offer, where no one knew or judged her. Where she could become just one of the crowd. Perth was just too small. Everyone knew everyone or was a friend of a friend. You couldn't go to the shops without bumping into someone you knew. Alice would hide behind her mother, begging her to stop talking so they could just go home. Alice's mum loved the gossip and took every opportunity to know what was going on all the time. If she only knew how much you can learn by just staying silent.

Chapter 3

Otto had nearly finished packing the last of his things. His three-month stay in Freo had been full of fun times, and he'd been able to earn enough money to continue his journey north. Broome would be his next stop, a job lined up in a local bar. More sun, sand and girls sounded great to him.

A beach resort town in the West's Kimberley region. Cable Beach offers a dramatic backdrop for late-night swims and camel rides. Avoiding crocs was always an issue, but he was up for the challenge. It's a tropical gateway to the north, one of the world's greatest wildernesses. Starting its days as a pearling town, bringing workers from Indonesia, Malaysia, China, Japan and Europe, much like Freo, he was excited to take in the town's multicultural vibes and learn more about Australia's First Nations people. The beautiful coastline contrasting with the red dirt of the desert. It was an amazing place for a holiday and even though he was there to work he was sure he would find the time to take in all the sights. Otto had applied for a few jobs and received calls back for all of them. They were desperate for workers, and Otto was more than happy to have a few to choose from. From restaurant work, fruit picking and tour guide work, any of them would have been a great opportunity for him.

He'd been in Australia for eight months. His working visa allowed only for a twelve-month stay. By working up north and completing rural work, he could extend the visa for up to five years. He wanted to make sure he got the most out of this opportunity. You never know when your circumstances will change, so best to make the most of it.

Everything about growing up in Germany was carefree and liberating for Otto. He loved the lifestyle as a child and had many fond memories. He was allowed to be adventurous and experiment with new things, never being restricted by his parents' worries or anxieties. It was very much learning from your mistakes, challenging yourself, and if you got hurt, you got back up and tried again.

It was a magical time; the forests were green and provided the play a child needed to exert so much energy.

His parents worked long hours, so it was not unusual for him to be out with his friends until dusk. Only slowing down to eat and recharge.

Christmas is huge in Germany all year round, with many houses keeping their decorations out long after the New Year had been celebrated. Otto's house was no exception. Heading into the forest every year, his father would cut them the perfect tree. It was one of Otto's favourite memories, one he had kept in his heart ever since their relationship had deteriorated dramatically.

It was on one such outing to get a Christmas tree that Otto became aware his mother and father may not be as happy as he first thought. Before heading into the forest, they had needed to stop for supplies. A lady approached them, done up to the nines, stopping his father in the street. He wasn't close enough to hear what was being said, but he was old enough to know what was going on. He knew from her body language and the way she held his hip whilst whispering into his father's ear that it wasn't right. He tugged on his father's shirt tail and was swatted away. He was mad at his father; this was their time. The only time he had his father's full attention for a full day, and he didn't want it ruined. Thirty minutes later, after witnessing the horrible display in front of the entire town, they were on their way again after he had watched the lady paw his father up and down, leaving bright red lipstick on his neck. Otto pouted in the passenger seat. He wished he was big enough to wipe the smug smirk off his father's face. How could he do that to his mother? Otto would never let her know; it would break her heart. He sat there silently for the entire car journey, not wanting to talk.

As quickly as his lousy mood appeared, it was gone once they got to the forest. Otto was in his happy place. They trapesed out through the rows of pines and spent a good hour searching for the best one. They laughed and joked, Otto savouring every minute.

Otto exceeded his parents' expectations when it came to school. He excelled at learning, he loved everything about it, and took him no time at all to pick up on new concepts. He was extremely intelligent.

When he was younger, he had many friends with whom he spent many long days adventuring, but as they grew older, they drifted apart. He withdrew from the group, becoming engrossed in his learning. Engineering had become his passion. Wanting and needing his father's approval, time with his friends became less of a priority, but at the same time, without noticing, he and his mother had become less of a priority for his father. Otto needed to succeed. He needed to be the best. He needed his father to see him.

His mother had been his greatest support, pushing him to excel. She was his greatest champion. Keeping him on track with his studies and never letting her emotions towards his father bubble over, he was her priority. Through everything, she was the rock. Keeping the family together and helping Otto move forward with his goals. Devastatingly, it wouldn't be long before this was all about to change for Otto.

Leaving Germany had been a relatively easy decision for Otto. He had been longing for change. His mother had passed away towards the end of his high school years. He remembered the day of the diagnosis, his father unable to look up from the table, his mother comforting his father, even though she was the one with the bad news. That was the problem; his mum was always the one holding it together, and without her, he knew it was the end of any family life he had ever known. His father had always worked, and his mother was the glue. Without her, there would be no home, no family. His father had never even cooked a meal.

Her death was slow and painful. It had broken Otto's heart to see her in such pain. Lengthy stays in the hospital away from home meant Otto had to learn to take care of himself fast. Trying to keep up with his studies and keep her comfortable had taken away most of his late teenage years. No parties or days at the beach were spent with friends. Friends? He wasn't even sure he had many true friends left. Otto had struggled to keep the few he had when his mum was sick. The main thing, though, was that he was able to keep up with his studies and end his schooling with good grades. Not that his father bothered to turn up to his graduation. He looked for him in the crowd and then realised, did he expect anything different? He'd hardly seen him when his mother was alive. Why would that change now?

His relationship grew distant with his father, his dad never being able to cope, and he drifted away even before his mother passed. Welcoming other women into the house less than a month after his mother was buried, for that Otto would never forgive him.

So, he made up his mind to travel to Australia. His father, already in a new relationship, didn't have much to say other than to keep in touch. Otto knew it would only be when he had to. His dad wasn't interested in him or small talk, so what was the point? He was determined to forge his own path. The one he had worked so hard for and sacrificed so much. Luckily for Otto, his mother had put money aside before she passed. She let Otto know she had saved it for him. Telling him to embark on an adventure while he was young, make the most of what the world had to offer. She had always dreamed of holidaying in Australia, so that's where he would start his journey. He remembered their animated conversations before she passed about all the things in Australia there was to do and see. His mum helping him plan his trip. Plenty of opportunity, sun, and surf. And maybe even some romance along the way. She had been so proud of his hard work and what he was to achieve. She wanted him to enjoy himself, finally.

Zipping his bag for the last time in Fremantle, he made a mental note to message his father in the morning just to let him know of his upcoming plans. The least he could do was let him know he was still alive, not that he expected a reply.

As he looked around his small room, Otto smiled, remembering his travels so far, after flying into Sydney last May, being amazed by the big city lights and the fantastic harbour bridge. It was a far cry from his small town back home. The friendliness of most Australians was contagious; the easy-going and carefree attitude appealed to Otto. He found it easy to pick up work in the many cafés that serviced the city – choosing one right in the centre of town, close to the one-bedroom apartment he had found for himself with the help of his mother's savings. The idea of a hostel was utterly horrifying to him. He was grateful not to be sharing a bunk or a bathroom. His first few weeks consisted of work and home; he felt like the four walls in the apartment would crush him. Worrying he had made a huge mistake, he had become very lonely. Luckily for Otto, his workmates looked out for him, and soon, they were inviting him to different places for catchups. The Australian BBQ culture was new to Otto. Sausages were a staple; the carb of choice was a steaming hot potato bake and, if you were lucky, a coleslaw for the obligatory hit of veggies. All finished off with many cold beers and a trifle or pavlova for dessert. If you were really lucky, a game of backyard cricket would bring out the competitiveness in everyone. For a German, this was very comical, especially when winter sports are all you've ever known.

A month into his Sydney stay, he met Anna and Heidi. Fresh off the plane, they had walked into his café. They were lugging huge backpacks similar to his own.

'Can I help you?' Otto smiled but abruptly stopped when he saw the panic on the girls' faces. 'Sorry, is everything okay?'

Heidi, the taller girl, looked up. 'We have just arrived, and our accommodation was incorrectly booked. We have nowhere to stay and no idea what to do from here.'

'Google is telling us everything is booked out.' Her voice croaked.

Otto could see they were both close to tears. He remembered what it was like not knowing anyone in a new city. He knew how hard it was to get the courage to ask a stranger for help.

'Please don't worry. I can help and if I can't I'll find someone else that can.'

Recognising his accent, the girls sighed with somewhat relief. It was a welcome sound in a foreign land.

'I'm about to finish up soon. If you want to wait, I can take you to find a place.'

Otto watched the girls' panic wash away, and they nodded eagerly.

'In that case, can we please get a coke each,' Heidi spoke first, relieved they had somewhat of a plan she needed a drink. The prospect of having to sleep rough on their first night in a strange city had frightened her. She didn't need to give her parents any excuse to fly her straight back home. They hadn't wanted her to go, but Heidi had been determined, and once she had convinced Anna to come with her, it was too late to turn back. Her parents had been overprotective all her life, and now Heidi finally felt like she could breathe. No way would she be calling them for help or letting on that there were problems.

As Otto went back and forth serving tables, he made sure to check in with the girls. From their conversation, they realized they had not lived far from each other back home. This was a great comfort to all of them. Otto, for the first time in a long time, was able to share warm memories of home. His heart still hurt from losing his mother, but he was hopeful his travels could help that.

Otto finished his shift and called for Heidi and Anna to follow him. He would first try the local hostel but knew it would only be a short-term solution until they found a job. Living in such close contact with people wore thin quickly, but it was the only choice they had at this point.

'It's nothing like what we had planned, but it will do for now,' Heidi said. 'Thank you, Otto.'

'It won't be long until you find work and can get something better. It took me less than a week to find work at the café.'

'Otto, we are so glad we walked into your café. I couldn't think of anything worse than having nowhere to sleep. We knew we might have to sleep rough at some point, but our first night would have been hell.'

'We are exhausted from the flight, but if it's okay with you, maybe you can show us around tomorrow.'

'Not a problem at all; I have the morning shift. Call past the café around lunchtime, and we will eat and head out to the harbour.'

'Thanks so much. That sounds great.'

Otto waved and left the girls to get organised. He had been happy to find new Aussie friends in Sydney. Now, having two new friends who shared his memories and stories of home would help him form a connection he knew was more significant than most – needing that human connection now more than ever after losing his mum was so important to him and his father now missing in action from his life didn't help.

The girls arrived in time to have a quick bite to eat before Otto finished his shift. He had to make a quick stop at his unit to change his shirt, which smelt like fried fish and chips, before they made their way to the harbour.

'Wow, this is nice, Otto.' The girls' eyes wide walking into his unit – a far cry from the backpackers.'

'I was lucky my mum left me some money before she died. It has helped me to get settled.'

'How long do you plan on staying in Sydney?' asked Heidi, picking up a photo of who she assumed was Otto's mother.

'I plan to do three to four months in each place I visit. If I have work to go to, I'm happy to travel anywhere.'

'Where will you go next?'

'In a couple of months, I'll start looking at jobs in Adelaide. It will be interesting to see how the cities differ.'

Anna looked up. 'Your mum is beautiful, Otto. I'm sorry she has passed.' Putting the photo down, she continued. 'Hopefully, we can get work soon, and maybe we can travel along to Adelaide with you. We don't have any set plans.'

'Sounds like a plan.' He smiled. It would be great to have the girls along on the adventure. 'Let's go check out the harbour. You will be amazed.'

Heading out, the threesome were all in high spirits. They couldn't think of a better way to spend your second day in town.

It would be three long months of hard work, fun and sightseeing before the three decided it was time to move on. Sydney had been a blast. The girls had managed to secure jobs in their first week at a local café. It hadn't been without its dramas, but they knew it was just a way of saving money to get ready for the next leg of their trip. Making the most of what Sydney had to offer, they spent their downtime exploring every inch, from the vast beaches to the inner-city culture. They had fallen in love with Australia, not missing anything from back home. Their families would try time and time again to coax them back, but they weren't interested. With their savings and Otto's, they were able to buy themselves a travel van they aptly named Betsy. Betsy was a bright red van painted to cover the red rust beneath. They were hopeful the weather would be kind enough for them to camp outside after realising three sleeping in the van may be a bit of a tight squeeze. Heading for Adelaide, they had formed a close friendship, and Otto had never felt more connected to people in a long time. Things looked bright, and Otto was excited for the adventures that lay ahead.

Chapter 4

I hate other kids. I can't be like them. I don't understand them. All the cutesy, wutesy crap, it's not for me. My mother hates me. She wants me in dresses and frills, and I can't bring myself to like it.

Pinks and purples, flowers and bows, just kill me now. She wants me to be normal. Whatever that is. I have to go along with it; I have to pretend. Sometimes, I want to go to my room and just scream, but I can't show emotion. I won't. I've learned how to turn it off. I can fake it when I need to.

My mother freaks out and tells my father she's seen it all before. She knows what I am. I don't know what she means, but the more I avoid her, the easier it is for me. When she makes me mad, my mind goes black. It's like I'm not in my body. I have become two different people. The Alice who pretends she's normal goes towards the light, and the real Alice lingers in the dark; it makes me want to keep my mum quiet permanently, for her never to wake up, to leave me alone. Luckily, my father is there to pull me back. I've found myself standing over her many times in the dark, wishing, willing her to die. One day, I know I will not be able to stop. Ruth will need to be put down. I won't have her making me feel like this for the rest of my life.

My mum comparing me to other kids causes so many problems. Parents talk, and kids listen. School isn't great, but I don't care. It's a means to an end, to escape this crappy place. Luckily, I'm left alone. The kids learnt quickly that I am not to be messed with.

But my mum looks at me like she knows what I am. I can't have that. Telling me constantly that I'm like him. I have no idea who 'him' is, but obviously, he's someone my mum has had problems with.

One day, I'll find out who he is, but I doubt he's like me. I'm yet to find anyone that is.

Abby Fletcher had been Alice's only friend all throughout their schooling. The Double A's they were known as. Mostly left alone by others but inseparable from each other. Finding similarities in themselves brought them closer together. They were each other's biggest comfort. Alice was surprised at the connection. After always being told she was weird, she never thought she would ever have any friends, and then there was Abby. The closest friend she would ever have.

It was Alice's first day at her new school, and she was nervous yet scarily calm. It hadn't been the first time her mother had her change schools, always worrying about what other people thought of her. Thinking she was the weird one and making her start all over again like it was a punishment. Little did she know Alice was not concerned. She wasn't worried about making new friends or fitting in. She didn't like anyone anyway. She just worked on not being seen and burying herself in learning. Alice was aware she needed to pretend, at least a little bit, that changing schools bothered her, or her mother would have her back at Dr Mary's office before she knew it. Her mother had long suspected there was more to Alice's shyness and unwillingness to be around others, but Alice quickly learnt how to play the game. She knew how to show just enough emotion to get her mother off her back.

'Hello.'

Alice heard a small voice behind her. A girl with blonde hair pulled tight into a high ponytail looked down at the floor before her. Averting her eyes from everyone around. Her tiny frame shrunk into itself. *If I sneeze, she will blow away*, Alice thought. Pale, she looked like she hadn't seen the sun in years.

'My name is Abby. I'm new too.'

'Hello, I'm Alice,' surprised she wanted to reply. She wanted to help Abby. There was something different about the mouse-like creature in front of her, drawing her in. Seeing herself in the big blue eyes now staring back at her. A complete opposite to Alice's dark, almost black, eyes and long brown hair. It was at that moment that Alice knew Abby needed her.

Abby had slowly lifted her head, eyes wide, not expecting Alice to have replied, just as Alice had surprised herself by replying. Slowly, a smile spread across both girls' faces, and without saying anything, they instinctively knew, they needed each other. The force was magnetic.

Their primary school was not very big, yet they both managed to get through relatively unnoticed, careful not to draw attention to each other. Their closeness did cause the other kids to avoid them. They were too close and too different for them to understand. Abby and Alice liked it that way. They only needed each other. There were times, though, when Abby realised just how much Alice needed her.

'Calm down, calm down, breathe, Alice,' Abby held her close, whispering in her ear. She could feel Alice shaking in her arms.

'Who cares what Bobby Mullins thinks? I know I'm adopted, and he is just a big jerk.'

'You shouldn't let him talk to you like that, Abby. He called us freaks!' Alice was furious. She could see Bobby taunting her from behind Abby.

Come closer, you wimp, Alice thought. *I'll show you what a real freak looks like.* Alice's insides were boiling, boiling over with pure hate. This wasn't her first time dealing with Bobby Mullins. He was a thorn in everyone's side. He was far too big for his boots. Someone needed to bring him down a few pegs.

Abby managed to calm Alice this time, but it was the times she wasn't there that worried her.

The last time they had argued with Bobby Mullins, the expensive trainers he got for his birthday had gone missing. He had spent weeks gloating and rubbing them in everyone's faces. Going on about how rich he was when he first got them, making some kids cry with his arrogance.

They were his pride and joy. Then they went missing, it sent Bobby insane. For weeks and weeks, they watched as he frantically searched for them. His mother was furious. Apparently, they weren't as rich as he wanted everyone to believe. Then, one day, they turned up out of nowhere, shredded into a ball of nothing. Bobby was devastated. It looked like they had been attacked with a chainsaw. Bobby broke down. Abby happened to catch a sideways glance at Alice. She had a smirk on her face. Something in that expression made Abby shiver. Her best friend scared her. Could it be that Alice was involved? Surely not, Alice had a temper, but this would be too far for even her. Or was it?

Chapter 5

Alice made her way back to her city hotel. A short walk from the train station in the quieter part of the city. She could see the Swan River from where she stood. Perth was far more beautiful than she remembered. She had hated the suburbs growing up, the identical brown brick houses, street after street with the same view. She had been happy to leave it all behind, but standing on that hill she realised it hadn't been all that bad. She still had her favourite memories of Abby.

Alice walked on, noting the security cameras as she went. That was the good thing about Western Australia being so slow to catch up with the rest of the country, let alone the world. It was yet to have security cameras on every corner. It still allowed for areas of privacy that those in other countries weren't so fortunate to have. Northbridge would be a challenge though. Camera surveillance was a must in that area where the pubs and clubs were open at all hours of the morning. It did provide a false sense of security for the late-night revellers, thinking everything would be caught on camera should something occur, which was often the case but not always. Alice had walked the streets of Northbridge many times over the years. She knew how she was going to come and go undetected. It had been tried and tested on many occasions when she wanted to avoid the crowds.

Alice had packed everything she needed in her hand luggage. She didn't want to be lugging a massive suitcase on a two-night layover. Serial Killing 101 suggested you don't want video evidence of you buying what you need in the same place as a dead body. Don't shit where you eat, was the Aussie slang for such an occasion.

Entering her hotel, she made her way upstairs, picking out her outfit. Knowing this would be the key to helping her get noticed. Men, she thought, were always the easiest prey for a pretty woman in a short skirt. Her hair was done, hanging long and straight down her back, almost reaching the centre, makeup on, just enough without overdoing it.

'Not bad, not bad at all,' she said aloud. Finally able to see what Abby had meant all those years ago. She hadn't wanted to be noticed back then; she couldn't believe anyone would ever find her attractive. She was the weird, unapproachable girl, but Abby had told her more than once she was wrong.

Walking down to the lobby bar, she made sure to make eye contact with an elderly couple in the lift. Giving the husband a cheeky wink as she exited. *First sighting,* she thought, looking at her watch, nine p.m. He wasn't likely to forget. His jaw almost hitting the floor was proof of that.

Making her way through reception, taking note of everyone she passed, making sure all eyes were on her, just as she wanted it. Now, patting herself on the back for her wardrobe choice.

'Nice to have you back.' Eric, the bartender, gave her a wink. 'The usual?'

'Hey, Eric. Yes, please, it's great to see you.' Alice was relieved Eric was on tonight.

'Expresso martini it is, then.'

Alice had stayed at this hotel many times on her work layovers. She had no choice, but it did allow for relationships to be made or, as she put it, character witnesses. She had many long late-night chats at the bar with Eric and, considering she liked no one, found it very easy to talk to him. She was always careful not to overshare and always kept her guard up, not letting him see the real Alice. Eric was your typical charming Aussie bartender, not sleazy, just able to put you at ease and make you feel important. He was good at his job – quite the lady's man. Alice couldn't help but feel special that he remembered her name and favourite drink every time she was there.

'Big night planned,' Eric asked, looking her up and down. *Good,* Alice thought. Eric noticed.

'I'm waiting to hear from some friends, but I won't be mad if I don't hear from them. I'm exhausted from this morning's flight.' A lie Alice knew needed to be told. It would help for her cover story later if she needed one.

Eric turned as more customers made their way to the bar. Alice knew Otto and his friends had planned to meet for dinner at seven p.m., and then make their way into

Northbridge, where they were meeting others at Paramount.

A large group of guys on a stag party entered the bar. Alice made sure to move seats, noting the looks she received and how many had now seen her at the bar.

'Great, so much for a quiet night.' Eric shook his head. 'Looks like it's about to get crazy.'

Crazy is an understatement, thought Alice. Things were about to get insane.

Chapter 6

The Double A's managed to remain unnoticed through most of their time at primary school. Abby managed to keep Alice grounded more times than not and had only seen a few glimpses of the Alice that made her scared.

One of those times was at Alice's house when they had walked in on her parents having an argument.

'It's not healthy, Peter. She needs more friends; she and Abby are too close, and it creeps me out. They even have the same mannerisms.'

'Really, Ruth, does it matter that much? They are happy together.' Her father sighed.

'Peter, I'm telling you something's not right; always hiding in her room, barely talking. It is weird.'

'God, Ruth, you'd think she was the devil the way you carry on. If you're that worried, book her into Dr Mary again, even though she has already told you she's a perfectly normal ten-year-old.'

'I know my daughter,' Ruth shouted. 'I have seen this behaviour before. I know what she is and what she is capable of.'

This had become more and more of a problem at Alice's house. Her parents argued about everything. If it wasn't her, it was something else, but her mother always seemed to come back to her. Her mother didn't understand her. She scared her. Abby and Alice entered the room just as her mother finished yelling.

Her mother turned back to the kitchen sink, furiously scrubbing imaginary dirt off the dishes. Her father kept his head in the newspaper, knowing her mother had gone too far but not game enough to stand up for Alice. The girls had heard everything. Abby had gripped Alice's hand tight, digging her fingernails into her palm. Alice knew she was trying to help her keep calm, it wasn't working. They headed for Alice's room without looking back.

'Alice, it's all right, you know your mum worries.'

'She doesn't need to!' Alice raged, trying to calm herself. No tears, Alice never let any emotion find its way to the surface. She would not allow herself to cry. She let herself calm down, knowing she would be at Dr Mary's tomorrow. Dr Mary had always been her mum's first point of call when she needed to whinge about Alice. Alice wasn't bothered. She had that old duck wrapped around her finger. By the time Alice was finished with her, her mum would look like the crazy one. Yes, this would be the last time she would be taken to Dr Mary. Abby glanced over just in time to catch Alice's smirk; she knew what was coming and it wasn't going to be anything good.

Chapter 7

By the time the three travellers made their way to Western Australia, they were old hands at all things backpacking. Adelaide had been a stepping stone to save money to get to Western Australia. Working in the amazing Barossa, with its Mediterranean climate and five-star retreats, almost didn't seem like work at all. Picking grapes and helping at the cellar doors was a fantastic experience. They learnt so much and met many wonderful people. Farm work was worlds apart from the city cafés of Sydney. Heading to bed early, waking before the sun was up. No nightclubs or all-night parties, Adelaide was a means to an end, and they had loved every bit of it.

Fremantle drew them in with the relaxed coastal vibe, plenty of travellers to make friends with, and an abundance of work and places to keep them entertained at night. It was here they would stay until Otto found himself with job offers for further north.

Otto finished the last of his packing and made his way downstairs. Anna and Heidi were meeting him at the restaurant after he dropped his bag at the bus depot. He was on the early bus; he knew that by dropping his bag now, it was guaranteed to be loaded even after a big night out. He didn't want to run the risk of leaving anything behind.

It would be hard to leave Anna and Heidi. They had work contracts to finish before they headed up to meet him. They would drive Betsy up afterwards; they could continue to use her while they stayed in Freo. Then she would be perfect for their stay in Broome. Otto had a room attached to the pub, and they had agreed the girls could park up Betsy out the back and use the bar facilities. They would not be paying rent which was a big help. They would be able to save ready for the next leg of their trip.

As he walked through the café strip, Otto waved to the many friends he had made, assuring them he would be back one day.

The bus terminal was very busy. Otto looked for the gate he would be departing from. He checked his bag and watched it be loaded into a nearby locker with the guarantee that it would be on the bus in the morning.

Otto was nervous about the trip, but he knew it was time to go. There was so much yet to see and explore, and he only had a limited time to do it in. His mother would be proud of him, and he wanted to stick to the plans they had worked on together.

Heidi and Anna made their way to the restaurant. They saw Otto approaching from the other direction. The noise of the café strip was deafening. Cars, buses, buskers, and people lining the streets made it hard to hear the person standing next to you, let alone someone across the road.

They jumped and waved to get Otto's attention.

'Otto over here.'

'Good to see you.' Otto took them in a big bear hug.

'I can't believe you are leaving tomorrow. It better go quickly for us, so we can get back on road to meet you.'

The girls looked at each other. It would be their first time without Otto's support since they came to Australia. They wondered how they would survive without him and his guidance.

'Let's not talk about it now and enjoy our last night as a threesome.'

They hugged. Tonight, would be a blast, the send-off their friend and brother Otto deserved. As close as they were, things had never been awkward between them, each knowing that the friendship was sacred, and boundaries were not to be crossed. They had their fair share of dalliances outside of the friendship threesome, making sure to be respectful of each other's space. In Adelaide, Anna had managed to find herself an Aussie cowboy working on a local farm. It was short lived but the other two weren't about to let her forget it. All in gest, they had laughed many times about waking early to see his boots sticking out of her bunk. For some reason he kept them on, even though everything else came off, the boots stayed, creating no end of amusement for the others. Anna had laughed along, knowing they meant no harm, but she had needed that closeness from someone. At times, their little friendship was claustrophobic, and an escape was needed. She couldn't always be the responsible one. She needed her space. Dave had been that escape, the larrikin she had needed to take her mind off work and off home. He had been kind and caring and good for a laugh. Just what the doctor ordered. Heidi's parents and her own were forever harassing them to return home. They did not understand the need to travel, to explore, or to leave their families behind. It was a different era; the girls were ready to take full advantage of it. They would see out their visas proving to themselves and those around them that they could succeed. Unlike Otto, school had not come easy, and their parents had been concerned about what would come of them. Both being down to earth and wise beyond their years would see them go far, a lot farther than their families expected or gave them credit for.

At the restaurant, they waited for their friends to arrive before ordering. A large group of about eleven, they stood out in the small room. Otto ordered a Pint and a Parmi, the Aussie pub staple. He'd served it many times at his café. The unspoken law of chips on the side, no salad, would just be a waste of greens. The group sat laughing and talking for a good few hours as the clock passed ten p.m. Many stories were told of their first meetings and what lay ahead in Broome. They were particularly interested in the stories of crocodiles on the beach. It left the girls thinking, was this such a good idea?

'By the time we get to Northbridge, it will be well past eleven p.m., peak time for the clubs.'

'Let's pay and get to the train station. I want to dance.'

Heidi lifted her hands above her head and cheered loudly, 'Great, here we go.'

Anna thought maybe that last drink wasn't such a good idea. Heidi was understandably drowning her sorrows at Otto leaving, but they still had a long night ahead.

They paid for their meal, then weaved their way through the crowd on their way to the train station. A wave of happy revellers followed behind, all headed for the same destination. Perth city, where the bright lights stayed on to all hours of the morning.

'What time does your bus leave?' one of Otto's mates from work asked.

'Leaves right at seven. I've got all my alarms set, but by the looks of it, I may just head straight to the bus after tonight. Worry about sleep when I'm on the bus.'

'Ha-ha, sounds like a good plan, mate.' With a slap on the back from his friend, Otto was ready to let loose. He needed to relax. He couldn't help but feel nervous. He needed to let go until tomorrow and then sleep through the nerves. He'd be passed out after enough drinks as soon as he hit the seat.

The train wasn't overcrowded, but like any train line in any country at any time of the day or night, the smell of all sorts permeated through the train cars. Body odour, urine, and stale beer are always a constant reminder not to touch anything. Luckily, there was no one on the train looking to make trouble, especially when they were all in for a fun night.

The vibe on the train was electric. Otto with his best friends and a bright future ahead. Broome was an amazing opportunity. He kept pinching himself at how well his trip had gone so far. Finally, he was feeling like he was someone, he was capable, and he was deserving.

'Remind me to message, Dad,' Otto called over to Heidi. Remembering his promise to himself to keep his father informed, even if his father wasn't concerned.

'Plenty of time for that, Otto, now come on, let's party.' Heidi was up off the train seat, shaking her head from side to side to imaginary music. Anna shook her head.

'Oh, Otto, it's going to be a long night,' Otto laughed. He loved these girls. They had come into his life when he needed them the most, and now, they were there to stay.

Chapter 8

Dr Mary's office was everything Alice hated about the world. Light, bright, girly, and full of flowers, it made her want to gag. She didn't need to be here. Her mother had once again dragged her in for no good reason. Playing on her own insecurities that had nothing to do with Alice. Today, Alice was ready to put on a show, play the game, if you will, and teach her mother a very valuable lesson. Don't mess with Alice Munroe. Don't interfere where it is not needed. She and Abby were best friends. They needed each other.

Sitting next to her mother, anyone else may have felt some guilt for what was about to happen, but not Alice. She had had enough; her mum should have left her and Abby alone. Abby was her best friend, closer to her than her family and the only person that mattered. No one would ruin that for her. Ever.

Dr Mary opened the door to her consultation room. Looking around, she called for Alice and her mum to enter. *Great,* she thought, *here we go again.* The helicopter parent with a bright kid who is worried they are on the brink of insanity. Give me a break. I can't believe they are back here again.

With some of the kids she had seen of late, this was a walk in the park. Alice Munroe was a victim of her mother's overthinking and trying to keep up with the Jones. Poor Alice, she could tell, had gone into her shell trying to appease her mother, only making her mother worry more. Her mother had gone to the extreme, creating an illusion in her mind of what or who her child should be. It wasn't real, and it wasn't fair to project such things onto a child.

Oh well, at $200 an hour, who was she to argue? Let's just sit and listen, and we can get through this.

'Hello, Ruth; hello, Alice, please come through, lovely to see you both again.' That was a lie. 'How can I help you both?'

'It's gotten worse, Dr: Alice won't talk to us, and she is constantly attached to her one friend, Abby. They are never apart, always whispering. It's creepy. She needs to branch out, make new friends and be more social. She needs to be like the other children. I have seen this behaviour before. I can't explain, but I know what is coming.'

Dr Mary looked at Ruth. Not believing what she was hearing. Is this woman worried about her daughter having a really good friend? If she only knew what she had to deal with every day. There were kids with no parents whose personality disorders had completely taken over them, kids riddled with anxiety, unable to function day to day. Those parents struggled to keep their kids alive. Kids who needed more support than she could give, and here was this woman with a perfectly healthy child trying to find fault.

Trying to get her to agree that her child has something wrong with her.

It was so hard not to roll her eyes. Dr Mary looked over at Alice.

'Alice, how have you been? Is there anything you need to talk about?'

'Hello, Dr Mary, I am fine, thank you for asking.'

'How do you feel about what your mother is saying?'

'It hurts my feelings. I'm lucky to have such a good friend; she likes me, and I like her.'

Ruth's jaw dropped; it was the most she had heard Alice say for months. This is unbelievable. What game is this child playing?

'Actually, Dr Mary, I am glad my mother brought me in today. I have been very worried about her.'

Alice's mum exploded. 'What are you talking about, you silly girl? We are here because you are not normal. I am not the problem here, you are! You creep me out, always sneaking about. All the other mums whisper about how strange you are, and how it's not normal to have only one friend. I can't live like this. I can't have them talking about my family like this.'

Alice started to cry; no tears, of course, but this was how she played the game. This is how she would get her mother to never interfere in her life again. Her mother was enraged. Never had she seen Alice show any emotion, let alone cry. She had no idea what was happening.

'You're a horrible child. What are you playing at?'

Dr Mary stood. 'Please give us a moment, Ruth. I want to speak to Alice alone.'

'I am her mother. You can't kick me out! You need to listen to me. I am the adult here.'

Dr Mary stood, pointing at the door. 'I'll ask you once more, Ruth, and then I'll call security. Please leave. Don't make this any worse than it is already.'

Ruth stood, looking back as Dr Mary watched her go. Looking back at Alice, Ruth could have sworn she saw her smirking.

Dr Mary turned back to Alice. 'Alice, is there more you would like to tell me about what's happening at home now that your mother has left the room?'

Alice nodded. 'Yes, lots more.'

Over the next thirty minutes, Alice went into great detail about all the problems she was having at home. Very little of it was true, but it's what Alice had to do. Her mother had forced her hand. From the fights with her father to always trying to make her talk and pushing her to make new friends, Alice left nothing out.

Dr Mary stood up. She'd heard enough. She'd committed people for less. How could a mother do this to her child? Even after all this, Alice had begged her not to put her mother away. Alice knew that having her mother committed was too extreme even for her. So, it was decided her mother would do a two-week break at a 'wellness centre' where she could take some time out to think about how lucky she was to have Alice as a daughter.

Victory, Alice thought. Never again would her mother dare meddle in her life. Never again would her mother question who she was. She had played the game and won.

Ruth couldn't believe what was happening, but the louder she got, the more she pointed and blamed Alice, the worse she made it for herself. No one would listen to her; they were treating her like she was insane. What the hell had happened? Her fears had made her sound like the crazy one, instead of making the situation better. All the commotion just cemented to Dr Mary that she had made the right decision. Ruth Munroe needed to give her child space.

Alice sat patiently waiting for her father. Dr Mary had rung him and explained the situation. With great relief to Alice, her father had agreed that things had not been great at home. He was quick to jump at the chance to have some peace from Ruth himself. He couldn't take the constant fighting any longer.

She watched as her mother was dragged away. In the end, not putting up much of a fight, maybe resigned to the fact that a break could be good for her. She knew she should feel bad, but that never came. Relief now that she would not be back here, relief that she and Abby could continue being friends in peace. No more accusations and no more accusing eyes. The town gossip and car park mums wouldn't be able to help themselves. They would have a field day with this. Her mother would be the talk of the town. Alice knew her mother would rather die than have them talking about her.

Oh well, she thought, *that could be arranged if push really came to shove.*

Dr Mary fussed over Alice until her father arrived.

What a day, she thought. Thank God that's over. At least she didn't have to deal with Ruth Munroe for a while. She was right where she needed to be. Away from her daughter, dreaming up problems that weren't there. Making her child feel less than others. Too many parents had free reign to destroy their children. Alice would not have to struggle any more. Well, at least for the next two weeks.

Chapter 9

Ruth Munroe had a very normal upbringing or so she had first thought. The sixties in Perth was a great time to be a child. Carefree days spent with friends, not home until the sun went down. Ruth was from a very large family, born right in the middle of seven kids. School wasn't a huge concern back then, and she found herself doing the bare minimum. Ruth was no fool, though, street savvy from a young age, forced to grow up quickly with older and younger siblings and parents who worked full-time. Their mum often worked two jobs to keep the large family fed and clothed. The kids were never aware of the hardships the family faced. It was all surf, sun, and fun for the kids. As long as there was bread, milk and Weetabix in the cupboard, the kids were full, content, and happy.

Ruth couldn't remember a time that she wasn't happy. They were one big happy family who always had each other's back. The kids at school knew not to mess with them. There was always an older one there to protect the younger ones. No one was game enough to take on the family, especially her brother Kevin.

Ruth's older brother, one above her, had been fiercely protective of Ruth ever since she was born, so much so that, at times, he had scared the other siblings. Something just wasn't right with how protective Kevin was. When he got that look, they all knew to back off. Nothing good would come of it.

Kevin was different. Ruth's father even kept a wide berth. No explosive temper or furious outbursts, just an underlying unease that left everyone on edge. He was the only sibling ever to have his own room. No one complained when he had asked for his privacy. He was loud and bashful, always had something to say, always wanting to be the centre of attention. His over-eagerness scared people. He was too out there, some even calling him unstable.

He hid his anger well. Never let it boil over, using his loud, obnoxious self to hide it, sarcasm becoming his go-to. No one challenged him. He ruled the roost.

Ruth loved him and knew he was her fiercest protector, but she also knew deep down that he was dangerous.

This is exactly what she would come to see in her own daughter. She knew the signs. She knew what was coming, and, in her rush to put a stop to it, she had ended up looking like the raving loony. Ruth knew what Alice was capable of, but when no one would listen, what could she do? She would need to wait now, bide her time and if it came to it, she would need to stop Alice herself. She had failed with Kevin and lost track of where he was now, but she knew he was still active. Now and then, she would pick up on a news report. His MO had become evident to her when they were young. She knew it off by heart now. She had followed his every move.

Ruth Munroe would not let her daughter fulfil her destiny, it was Ruth's bad DNA that had got her here, and it was up to Ruth to stop it.

Kevin loved life; he loved his family, especially his little sister Ruth. Nothing stood in his way. He knew people gave him a wide berth; he was too loud and too aggressive at times, and his temper often got the better of him. He was seriously intimidating. Kevin wasn't used to not getting his own way. It rarely happened, but if it did, he found himself fighting to control his anger. He was Kevin Angelo. He demanded respect.

Kevin made sure Ruth had no idea how their family struggled. Ruth had no idea of her father's drinking issues and the abuse her siblings had suffered from him. He was prepared to take the brunt of his father's anger to keep the others safe especially Ruth.

A fierce drunk, their father consumed their mother with fear. Kevin would never let Ruth see. To her, their father could do no wrong. Her family was perfect.

Several times, when he was younger, Kevin was pushed too far. It took all his strength not to lash out. His inner strength would eventually not be enough to stop his urges.

Leaving home had been heart breaking for Kevin. Ruth was still too young to leave with him. He was worried about how he would protect her. He found a newfound freedom to become more himself. To grow and nurture the darkest parts of his soul. The parts he had kept hidden from all, even Ruth.

Ruth could remember the terrible tragedies that surrounded her brother, first their father and then friends and girlfriends. People he had loved dearly seemed to meet untimely deaths. Ruth's heart had broken for her brother, but then again, unfortunately, bad luck seemed to follow him.

Kevin had left home in his late teens to live with his friends, leaving behind years of torture from his father. Even though his father gave him a wide berth, he still found himself at the end of a beating, stepping in to protect his siblings. Angry at his mother or just looking for a fight, Kevin was always there to step in, taking a punch or two.

Now out of home, they no longer had his protection. Ruth had called a few times, worried about their mother. She had been at the end of a beating, and Ruth had witnessed it for the first time.

Kevin would not let his father continue to torment his family. He was a worthless pig, and it was time he was stopped. This was the first time Kevin would have the opportunity to stalk and follow through with a kill. He had fallen short many times, knowing his family relied on him. Now, they relied on him to finish this. Watching his father leave work, he could have put money on the direction he would choose, of course, heading in the direction of the pub and not the family home.

'Well, no one can say he isn't a creature of habit,' Kevin muttered.

He wouldn't need to rush. He knew his father would be a good few hours. Talking crap with his alcoholic pals, all avoiding having to go home for one reason or another. He never really knew why his father didn't want to come home. Was it the financial pressures, or was it the seven children? Either way, none of the kids had deserved this.

The sun set as Kevin slumped in the front seat of his car, waiting and watching. This had been a longer wait than first thought. His father was putting in a bigger session than usual.

The cars in the car park started to clear out until only two or three remained. Kevin waited. The door of the pub flew open as his father fell out backwards, stumbling in the dirt. Kevin got out of his car, taking big strides in the dark, getting to where his father lay before, he could get to his feet. He lifted him from behind under his arms, dragging him around the side of the building. Neither of them said a word, his father too drunk to realise what was happening. He looked up at Kevin, that look, he knew that look, he knew what was coming.

Pulling a knife from his back pocket, Kevin took one long last look at the pathetic human in front of him. His heart rate didn't change. His mind was blank. He now knew at that moment that he was born for this. Grabbing his father by the hair, not saying a word, he pulled his head back, exposing his throat. Pausing for theatrics, he almost asked him if he had any last words, but he didn't care enough to want to listen to the reply. Taking the knife, he slashed left to right against his father's throat, not enough to kill him, just enough to see complete fear in his eyes. Throwing him to the ground, Kevin looked at the sorry state in front of him, gripping his throat. Nothing escaped his mouth. This was his big bad father. Kevin came down hard and drove the knife into his chest over and over, releasing pure rage. Releasing himself of all the anger that had built up in his childhood. He could faintly hear his father gargling, but he made no effort to fight back. Kevin's anger raged on until his father's hands fell from his throat. He was gone. Kevin almost couldn't stop; the body was a mangled, bloody mess. Nothing but a picture of pent-up hate and rage.

Snapping back to reality, he could hear voices coming from the car park. Luckily, he was far enough around the corner in the shadows not to be seen or heard. He dragged the body towards the large green bin and dumped it inside. He made sure to cover any footprints and erase any sign that he was there. Taking the knife, he cleaned it on his father's shirt and threw it in the bin. Kevin at least had the sense to cover his tracks at this moment. He could no longer hear voices, so he took the opportunity to head back across the car park to his car.

Sitting in the driver's seat, he felt himself exhale, exhilaration and slight arousal building up inside him. It was only the start for Kevin. A spark had been lit, and there was no way he was ready to let it snuff out any time soon. He felt alive!

The next day, Kevin arrived at the family home just as they were receiving news of their father. They were devastated, distraught, not believing what they were hearing, all but Kevin were in complete shock. Ruth looked up just in time to see Kevin smirk. Surely, not Kevin, he was her closest family, and she loved him, but at this moment, she was more frightened of him than ever.

Chapter 10

As the hotel bar started to fill with more people, Alice checked the time. Almost eleven p.m., she would need to head back to her room shortly, but not before everyone caught one last look at her and hopefully the time.

'One last drink, please, Eric, before I go.'

'Have you heard from your friends?' Eric walked over.

'No, and I'm not bothered. I'll head upstairs and get room service. I still haven't eaten, and I'm starving.'

'One last drink coming up then.'

'Thanks, Eric.'

Alice drank the last of her drink, keeping a close eye on the time, and waved goodbye to Eric. Game on.

Making sure all eyes were on her as she left, taking the long way back to the elevator. As far as they all knew, she was heading straight back to her room to turn in for the night.

Back in her room, she prepared herself. She packed her backpack and got changed. Old jeans, a ripped shirt, and a dirty bomber jacket. Hair up in a tight bun tucked neatly under a cap. All remnants of makeup were wiped from her face. To anyone else, she would look like any twenty-something white male. No one would know. No one would care.

Once she was organised, she made a call to room service.

'Hi, this is Alice in room 102. Can I get a burger and the chocolate cheesecake, please?'

'No problem, that will be fifteen minutes, Miss Munroe,' the voice on the other end replied.

'Thank you. Can you bring it in and leave it on the table, please? I'm just jumping into the bath.'

Alice waited precisely thirteen minutes and turned on the tap in the bath, just enough so they could hear the water running. She needed them to believe she was in there just in case something went wrong with her plan.

She slipped quietly out of her room, heading for the back stairwell. Head down, avoiding looking at any cameras. Counting the steps as she went, knowing there were two hundred thirty-two before she hit the ground floor. She had done this many times, not wanting anyone to know her comings and goings, as she made it to the back alley and checked the time: eleven thirty, right on time. Cautiously, she opened the door, checking that no one was in the alley. As always, it was completely empty, giving her the perfect escape.

Counting the stops to Perth, the group couldn't wait to get there. Otto had sat quietly, excited for what was to come, but also felt the dread of having to leave his friends, the family he had yearned for so long. They were right there with him, and now he was leaving them.

It won't be for long, he thought. You can do this. It will all work out. At least if he got wasted tonight, he could hop straight on the bus and sleep the first leg to Broome, not having to think about it. Not having to worry, he had made a mistake. It was a great opportunity.

A voice came over the loudspeaker, 'Next stop, Esplanade Perth.'

'Finally! We're here. Thank God I need a drink or thirty,' yelled Heidi. Anna could tell she was in for a big night, mostly making sure Heidi didn't get herself into trouble.

Stepping off the train, they headed for Paramount. Located in the heart of Perth's nightclub district, Paramount is one of Perth's best. A massive club with industrial accents, disco balls, and dramatic lighting, where bands and resident DJs come to play. It was easy to get lost in that place and lose track of your friends. Heaving with people, it was a wait to even get close to the bar for a drink.

Taking her time, Alice made her way through the city, head down, blending in with the many homeless people who spent their nights wandering the streets, not wanting to lay down their heads in the dark for fear of theft and violence. Northbridge could be very volatile. Young people full of booze out to all hours of the morning was never a good combination.

No one looked her way, their eyes down, worried she would accost them for a smoke or coins. To them, she was invisible. A blight on society that the big cities wanted to pretend didn't exist. The total opposite of the person just half an hour ago in the hotel bar who wanted to be seen. Who had commanded attention.

The plan was to sit on the dimly lit footpath and wait. Not much of a plan at this point, but it would come together. There was a small ally opposite the club. From there, she would see everyone coming and going, staying in the shadows. She had a clear view. Each person needed to line up and be scanned in. This meant the line would be long and slow, meaning no one could sneak in without her seeing. She only had to wait about fifteen minutes before she saw the large group making their way to the entrance. She spotted Otto straight away, with dark hair and broad shoulders, the girl's white hair glowing in the streetlights.

Poor Otto, she thought. Not because of what she was about to do but for the pain she knew he was in. He was estranged from his father; his mother was dead. Alice could see the lost boy behind the big blue eyes. No amount of smiling or happy conversation could hide that. Alice knew that feeling, needing to be needed, wanting to be wanted. Alice couldn't let this go. She could feel the burning. It had to be done.

Chapter 11

Heading into high school, Alice and Abby had new struggles to face. Boys being one of them. Alice hated the attention Abby was getting from boys; Abby was changing.

The girls would walk to school together every morning, passing the same suburban houses as they went. Alice would set off from home and collect Abby on her way past. As Alice rounded the corner, she could see Abby talking to a boy at the bus stop. Alice felt a brooding below as she got closer and closer to Abby. What was going on? Abby spoke to her and only her. She didn't like this. Not at all.

Abby looked up just as Alice got close. She knew that look. She needed to get to Alice quickly.

'Abby,' snapped Alice, 'we are going to be late.'

Great, here we go, thought Abby.

'Sorry, Alice, I'm coming.'

Alice looked behind just as Abby waved goodbye to the boy.

This isn't right. This isn't right at all, thought Alice. Abby was her friend. When did boys become the thing that might come between them?

Abby wasn't the only one the boys had started noticing. Alice became increasingly uneasy as she was asked more and more times to go lab partners by different boys. She always thought it was because they wanted good grades, never realising how she was changing physically. Tall and willowy, with long dark hair and dark, brooding eyes, Alice was oblivious to her looks. She had no idea about fashion or makeup. She had struggled with all things girly since her mother had been on her little break. That two-week break had turned into two years. Alice and her father received a letter that her mother would not be back. Sighting the lack of support from her father in getting Alice the help she needed as her excuse not to come home. Choosing instead to leave them behind and move on with her life. At the time, Alice was pleased it had worked out far better than she ever thought it would.

She had not been concerned then, but she now faced the problem of navigating all things girly on her own.

She and Abby would often sneak down to the local deli, searching for the new Dolly magazine. Australia's number-one teen magazine with fashion, beauty, dating and life advice. Some stories left them gobsmacked. How would they ever know how to do any of those things? Would they ever want to? What Alice did know was that she was not ready for any of that at all.

Abby, however, showed far more interest and of course, she still had her mother to talk to about things. Plus, her interest in boys was far more advanced than Alice's.

Oh well, Alice thought, that was one sacrifice I made when wanting Abby to myself. No interference from my mother, but now, it would be other interferences to worry about.

A few years passed peacefully and relatively uneventfully. Alice studied hard and Abby trailed dutifully behind. Alice was committed to her studies and barely noticed Abby starting to drift towards more exciting things. She had started to make more friends and expand her circle. Alice was determined to get out of boring Perth, to see the world and have new adventures. It was obvious to her that the easiest way to do all this was to become a flight attendant. She was always fascinated by the well-dressed ladies she saw on TV flying to all sorts of exotic locations, all while being paid and living the high life.

Abby wasn't concerned with such high ambitions; she was very content in her little leafy suburb and the first family home she had ever known. She had become more and more aware of just how different her life was compared to Alice's and how much Alice wanted to get out of there. This hurt and scared Abby, but she dared not say anything to Alice. She guessed Alice thought she would just follow along like she always did. Abby wasn't so sure anymore.

She loved her family and couldn't imagine moving away. Abby had been a child who started her life not being wanted, shuffled around at an early age, eventually finding her forever family. She wasn't about to give that up in a hurry, not even for Alice. Her early years were the reason she was a little mouse when she met Alice, scared to stand out, scared to show anything in case her family didn't want her anymore. She knew she could help Alice when they first met after learning all those years ago how to keep herself calm. Now, she had grown, and something was telling her she could keep going without Alice. She would be fine. It was Alice she wasn't so sure about. Could Alice move on without her?

Turning the corner, headed to her locker, Alice walked straight into Gary. Tall, ash blonde hair, very athletic, not that Alice had ever noticed. She knew he was very smart and gave her a run for her money in science. He had been her lab partner a few times, and I guess the good thing was she didn't hate him, but nothing he had to say interested her. She was very competitive, and Gary proved to be quite the competitor. Alice was intrigued but not enough to want to instigate a conversation. Poor Gary stuttered, unsure how to approach talking to Alice.

'Oops, sorry, Alice, I didn't see you there.'

No problem let's keep this short, she thought. Alice wasn't one for small talk, especially with a boy.

'I've been meaning to ask; do you like the beach?'

Oh god, no, Alice cringed. The sand, the sun, she couldn't think of anything worse. People crowded on boiling hot sand with no shade was her worst nightmare. Well, one of them.

'Alice loves the beach; she was just telling me the other day about how she wanted to go.'

Alice turned to see Abby. *What a traitor!*

'That's great. A group of us are going on Saturday. Do you want to come?'

'That sounds like fun, doesn't it, Alice?' Abby answered for Alice, and Alice gave her the death stare.

'Okay, I'll see you there, bye, Alice.'

As Gary walked away, Alice grabbed Abby.

'What was that about? I hate the beach and hate people even more.'

'C'mon, Alice, please, I want to meet new people, and I think it will be good for you too. If you're going to be an air hostess, you at least need to learn how to pretend to be nice to people.'

Alice couldn't argue with that, thought Abby.

Unfortunately, Abby had a point that was the one obstacle that Alice knew was in the way of her escape plan. Learning how to have a fully-fledged conversation with an actual person was going to be a problem.

'I'll give it an hour, but don't even think I'm going near the water.'

'Thanks, Alice.' Abby danced down the hall with happiness.

Alice didn't even own a bathing suit; she would have to borrow one from Abby. What the hell was she thinking? Argh, and she'd have to shave. Being a girl was so time-consuming Alice would rather be doing anything else than having to worry about shaving.

Dreading Saturday, Alice avoided Gary as best she could for the rest of the week, even making sure she went in last to science once everyone was already partnered up.

She had tried a hundred times to get out of going, but uncharacteristically, Abby was standing firm. Abby was determined to get Alice out and about.

Alice started to slowly see the changes in Abby. She knew she had made new friends and was hiding them from her. Not home when she would call, or more and more times, already gone to school before Alice got to her house. Alice had been mad, very mad, but unlike every other time, she didn't have Abby to calm her down. She didn't want to confront Abby. They never fought; she didn't want to upset her. For the first time in their friendship, she had felt Abby was pulling away.

She had to learn to control herself without Abby, not letting the dark thoughts bubble over. Not letting herself lose control. Flicking the elastic band on her wrist, Alice felt herself calm. The instant pain of it took her mind back to her normal. Dolly Doctor had been very helpful with calming techniques.

Thank the devil for that magazine, Alice thought. It had been her saviour. It had taught her how to calm down without needing Abby there for support. She knew at some point Abby wasn't going to be there forever, so she had to learn how to do it herself.

Saturday came around fast. Abby had caught Alice after school on the walk home Friday.

'Make sure you get to my house early. You need to get the bathers.'

'Why are you so excited about this? I just want to die.'

Really, Alice thought, *wow, that's a bit dramatic even for you.*

'Please, Alice, please do this for me, just this once. Mark will be there, and please don't be mad. I like him,' Abby grimaced, waiting for Alice to reply.

'I'll see you at nine.'

As Alice walked away, Abby couldn't help but notice her flicking an elastic band on her wrist.

That's new, she thought. Something she'd never seen her do before now but something that would become more and more noticeable.

Chapter 12

Alice knew she would have to sit in the dark waiting for a few hours. She was more than prepared for this part. She had sat and waited in the shadows many times before. Making herself invisible in her surroundings. She had made sure she had everything she needed. A shopping trolley sat just out of sight, filled with rugs and cardboard. A staple for any homeless person on Perth streets. Even though it was summer, no one wanted to sleep on hard pavement. She sat there thinking, thinking of why this was so important to her, why she could not stop the compulsion. Why it needed to be done. There was no simple answer. It had always just been this way. For as long as she could remember, the dark thoughts ruled her, and once that burning in her stomach met her dark thoughts, there was no going back. It couldn't be stopped; the pull was too great. Somewhat opportunistic and somewhat planned but never stalking like this, stalking was very new to her. This feeling had only happened two times before, where she could not turn it off, where she had to see it through. Once in high school and once in her early twenties. They hadn't stood a chance.

Inside the club, hidden away from Alice, the drinks were flowing. The crowd was dancing. Otto was dancing, forgetting his worries for the time being. With one eye on the time, Otto knew he had about four hours before he'd have to head for the train. He didn't want to miss the bus. Oh well, he thought he had plenty of time for more drinks.

Heidi and Anna sat in a booth towards the back of the club. Heidi was feeling a little worse for wear after too much Yaeger and shots. Anna had suggested they take a seat before being cut off from the bar. Nothing ruined a good night more than being cut off.

'I'm going to miss Otto,' Heidi said, clearly emotional from all the drink. She could hear the words slur from her mouth. Oops, maybe she had had enough.

'I know, I know, but it won't be long until we meet up with him again. Betsy will get us there. We can stop at a few places on the way and have a bit of a holiday. We've done nothing but work.'

'I don't like not having him around. Who will look after us?'

'We have each other, Heidi. We made it to Australia without him. I'm sure we can last a few months. We will be on the road before we know it.'

'I know, I know; in that case, we need champagne,' Heidi slurred.

'I think I better go alone, or they won't serve either of us.' Anna stood and headed for the bar. Otto glanced over and saw Heidi slumped in the booth; he made his way through the crowd.

'You're not ready for bed already, are you?'

'No way, Otto, Anna has just gone for champagne. We were just saying how much we will miss you.'

'I will miss you both too. It will go fast, I promise. I may not be able to contact you until I'm sorted, and I'm hoping my phone works up there, but as soon as I can, I will call you both.'

'It will be okay, Otto; we know where you are. Betsy will bring us to find you.'

Heidi gave Otto a huge squeeze, how he loved these girls. They had been his constant support for so long now he was even worried about how things would go, but he wasn't about to let on to Heidi, especially in her current state. Thoughts suddenly wandered home; he remembered he had to message his father when he was on the bus. As the thoughts of home crept in, Otto found himself brimming with emotion. His mother had also been his constant support, and he'd lost her, his father not even bothering to call him. *Oh no, oh no, you don't. Let's not get emotional now. Hold it together.* Making sure to hide his face from Heidi. *Hurry up, Anna, where's that champagne?*

Alice had worked out that Otto would need to think about leaving at five a.m., which would get him back to Fremantle and the bus on time.

Only a few more hours, she thought. It had been an interesting night watching everyone from the ally. If only they could see each other. The drunk antics forgotten by the morning would have been enough to put you off drinking again forever. Girls spewing in the gutter, friends holding their hair back. Sitting on the curb crying, so many emotions.

Thank God I don't have those, Alice thought. Men bumping chests with each other, trying to prove who was more macho, apparently thinking taking your shirt off was a sure-fire way to make you look the toughest.

Just cringe worthy, thought Alice. If she wasn't waiting for Otto, she would have had plenty of volatile idiots to choose from to do in. How could any of them think this made them attractive to others? The power of alcohol was always fascinating. Not only did it erase your memory by morning, but it also made everybody look incredibly attractive, even with their head in a gutter.

No thanks, thought Alice. It's a no from me.

Just then, she noticed a few people from Otto's group leaving the club, some trickling out together and others alone. They all looked very unsteady as they went. This looked promising. The less steady they are, the easier they fall. This would be easy, but it had thrown her timeline out. She needed to think fast to adjust; now was not the time to panic. She had to be ready for Otto. Ready to end his pain.

Alice had no intention of making Otto suffer. He had suffered enough. That was not how she worked. Inflicting torture on someone was not her thing. It didn't excite her. Her excitement had come from the chase and, in this case, the knowledge that she was helping someone out of their misery or sparing the misery of others from someone else. This had been the case twice before. People who couldn't keep themselves to themselves. People who had forced her hand forced her to take them out. She had done the world a favour.

Shaking the thoughts from her head, Alice went back to concentrating on the entrance. More people were filing out now, all looking significantly worse for wear. It didn't take long for Alice to notice more of the group leaving.

This was earlier than expected, Alice thought. Heidi made her way out, held up by another male friend. She was totally incoherent, and the guy was struggling to hold her up. Holding her shoes in one hand, head hanging over his shoulder.

Let's hope that guy has good intentions, Alice thought. Not your problem, not now anyway. No Otto or Anna to be seen. Maybe they will stay later than the others, making Alice's plan run right on time.

Inside, Anna grabbed Otto's arm.

'I'm going to the toilet. Then we need to go. You can crash at ours for a few hours before the bus if you want. It's earlier than I thought it would be.'

'That might be a good idea. Staying out till five a.m., was a little ambitious.'

'Okay, you head outside, and I'll meet you at the kebab shop. I need food.'

As he stood, Otto realised just how much he had drunk. His legs were a little shaky underneath him.

'Woah, I don't feel so great.'

'You go and get food, and I'll meet you there. You will feel so much better.'

Otto wasn't so sure about that, but he set out one foot in front of the other. Was that one step or two? Otto laughed. He really was drunk. As he got to the entrance, he made his way slowly out onto the path, careful not to wobble or lose his footing. Leaning on the pole outside, he looked up and down the street. Oh, good, the kebab shop. I need a wee.

I'll use the ally next to it, he thought. The street had gotten a lot quieter as they had all started to make their way home. He tried to make his way to the kebab shop as best he could. Walking in a straight line wasn't that easy after twenty different drinks.

Otto. Alice spotted him the second he stepped outside. Unsteady on his feet, looking up and down the street. This was the part where Alice had to rely completely on human nature alone. She knew the lure of the kebab shop after a big night out was too great for most to resist. A well-known hangover cure, or so they all thought. That's another superpower of alcohol. The call of kebabs and salty chips was uncontrollable.

Alice crouched, slowing her breathing, not wanting to move a muscle in case it startled Otto. A couple walked by, obscuring her view, their tongues stuck so far down their throats that she was sure she heard them choking.

Gross, get a room. Damn it, Alice thought, hurry up and move. They finally moved, and Alice saw Otto had staggered closer, laughing and talking to himself. That's it, that's it, just a bit closer. As if reading her mind, Otto straightened suddenly and took a few steady strides, putting Alice off guard, by walking straight towards her and the ally. She hadn't planned for this; she had thought that once he had ordered from the kebab shop, he would come outside to wait to give her the opportunity to grab him, but now he was headed straight for her. Getting herself together, Alice waited. Slowing her breathing again, she tucked herself further and further into the shadows. Otto made his way into the ally. He was right in front of her now, fiddling with his fly.

Ah, Alice thought, *that's why.* Alcohol also played havoc on one's bladder. She waited as he finished his business. He staggered around, fumbling, struggling to do up his fly. Alice stood, startling Otto. He had not noticed anyone under the bundle of clothing hidden in the dark.

'Hello, Otto, I've been waiting for you.'

Chapter 13

The sun was just peeking through the curtains as Alice opened her eyes.

Oh crap, it's Saturday, she thought. *What have I got myself into?* Laying there looking at the ceiling, she wondered if it was a good idea to call Abby and tell her she was sick. Abby may never forgive her if she did. Then there was Gary, a whole other story. She had successfully managed to avoid him all week after bumping into him at the lockers. Not being one for social situations, Alice was unsure how to take Gary's attention. Firstly, believing it was for her brains only and now the awkwardness of feeling it was something more. By all accounts, Dolly Doctor magazine was telling her Gary was interested in more than just her brains, bringing a nauseous feeling every time Alice thought about it. She did not need the distraction. The sooner she was out of Perth, the better. *What the hell am I going to do if he talks to me? I don't do small talk.* Sighing, Alice thought the only way to get through it would be to pretend. She would need people skills if she were to become a flight attendant, so she would put that to good use today. With a huff and puff, Alice got up. She packed her bag and trudged down the hall. Grabbing the most enormous sunhat she could find to hide under.

'Where are you off to?'

Alice jumped, grabbing her chest. She hadn't seen her father in the lounge.

'Dad, you scared me! Just to Abby's and the beach.' She saw her father's jaw drop.

'I'm fully aware I am not a beach person, Dad,' she snapped more than she wanted to. Her dad had been so good to her over the years, giving her the space she needed.

'Wow, the beach, this is new, okay well, good for you.' He turned back to reading his paper, feeling quietly triumphant. Maybe getting rid of Ruth was a good idea after all. Alice was thriving.

Little did he know Alice's newfound confidence in the beach was to be short-lived. Accidents happened all the time at the beach. Today would be no exception.

Alice stepped out of the house and headed towards Abby's. He was far too enthusiastic about this situation, just like Abby. Argh, the pressure to like today was getting to her. Now she had to put on the dreaded bathers. Abby flung open the doorway, too excited for Alice's liking and this time of the morning. It was too early for fanfare.

'Settle down, Abby; I'm still not excited about today.'

'I know, Alice, and I appreciate you doing this for me. Mark has already messaged, and I'm trying hard not to act desperate. I really want him to like me.'

Well, you're not doing an excellent job at that, Alice thought.

'Let's get you into those bathers and see what they look like.'

Alice cringed, 'All right, all right.'

Heading into the bathroom, Alice wondered if it was worth jumping out the window and escaping.

Just get on with it, she thought; *with any luck, these won't fit, and I'll have an out.*

Stepping out of the bathroom, Abby's mouth gaped.

'See, I told you this wasn't a good idea; I look like a toad, don't I?'

'Omg, Alice! You look amazing!'

Alice hadn't even bothered to look in the mirror, but she was sure it was nothing to get that excited about. She turned and looked, surprising herself.

'Well, I wouldn't go that far, but at least they fit.'

'Damn you, Alice, you really can't be that oblivious. You have no idea, do you? You can't see what everyone else sees, and then you make yourself totally unapproachable, yet all anyone wants to do is approach you. Here I am screaming for attention, and you're totally oblivious you're getting it.' Abby huffed.

Don't push me, Abby, thought Alice, boiling inside. This was a huge thing for her, and making a big deal out of it wasn't helping. She turned for the bathroom and chucked her sundress over the top. She felt much better, hiding under all the material.

Abby knew she was brooding, but saying more would not help. Just let her calm down, and we can enjoy the rest of the day.

An hour later, Alice had gotten her head around the plan for the day. They headed out, passing the identical suburban houses they passed daily, this time walking towards the train station. Alice looked up to see Mark walking towards them. Abby was next to her, waving and flapping like a goose. Great, she didn't know he was travelling with them.

Alice was glad for the big hat she had worn. The sun was hot. 'I hope you girls have sunscreen,' Mark called out. 'It's a hot one.'

'I hope you do, Alice; your lily-white skin will burn to a crisp,' Abby whispered.

It was true Alice was white as a ghost, but not liking the great outdoors did that to a person.

Mark was closer now. 'Hey, Abby... Hey, Alice.' There was a notable pause between Hey, Abby and Hey, Alice. Were people really that unsure of her?

'Let's get to the beach. Everyone is waiting for us.'

They headed out past the industrial area and down towards the train line. It was a short trip into the city and then on the Fremantle line to Cottesloe Beach.

Cottesloe Beach is pretty as a picture. One of Perth's top beaches and most iconic for swimming, surfing, and watching gorgeous sunsets, not to mention gorgeous people. On a day like today, the beach would be heaving with people. *Good,* Alice thought, *I can blend into the crowd.*

Getting off the train, it was a short uphill walk lined with coastal pines. At the top of the hill, the coast stretched out before them, blue and inviting. Hundreds of people scattered the sand, looking like tiny ants from up on the hill. The many cafés were bursting out the doors, people wanting drinks, ice creams, and the forever iconic fish and chips at the beach.

The three of them made their way over to where their friends were on the grass. Some Alice recognised, some she didn't.

That's fine, she thought, *not like I'll be talking to anyone, anyway.* Gary came running out of the water, big broad shoulders glistening in the sun. *Alice Munroe, eyes down*, she commanded herself. Alice hid behind Abby and Mark.

'So glad you guys came; how good is the weather?'

'It's so nice, thanks for inviting us,' replied Abby. Alice kept her head looking directly at the sand; she didn't bother to look up. Why was she so awkward? Gary was perfectly pleasant. She just couldn't bring herself to chat with him. They made themselves comfortable on their towels, ready for a relaxing day. Even the sand was scorching hot. Alice, under her huge sun hat, stuck her nose straight into a book. At least she could catch up on her reading and not waste the whole day.

'Oh, look at this geek; what's the weirdo doing here? Who invited her?' Alice looked over to see Bobby Mullins looking and pointing in her direction.

Not this idiot again, sighed Alice.

'Go away, Bobby, find someone else to annoy.' Gary was behind her. She hadn't noticed he'd been lying on his towel.

'What's it to you, Gary? You got something going on with this geek.'

'I've said it once already, Bobby, shut your mouth and go away,' as he spoke, Gary stepped forward, and to her surprise, Bobby backed away. This was new; Bobby Mullins never backed down, but Alice could see for the first time just how much more significant and domineering Gary was compared to Bobby. Unlike Bobby, Gary commanded attention.

'Whatever, Gary.' Bobby always had to have the last word; he skulked away, kicking up sand in Alice's direction as he went. She could feel him staring her down but paid no attention.

'Sorry about Bobby, he really is harmless, just has a fat mouth sometimes; I am glad you came.'

'Harmless, yeah, right. Isn't that what they say just before a dog bites someone's face off? Oh, it's okay, he's harmless! Yikes, Alice Munroe, that was too far even for you.' Gary looked shocked.

'He's really not that bad.'

For the first time in her life, she heard herself say sorry. 'He gets on my nerves; he has hurt Abby so many times I've lost count. I didn't mean to be so abrupt. Thank you for telling him to stop. As you can tell, I might not have been so diplomatic.'

'It's okay. I understand he can be rude and get in your face, but I like to think there's no nastiness in it. Now are you sure you don't want to come for a swim? Forget about Bobby.'

'Give me a minute. I'll think about it.' Gary stood and headed for the water.

'You'll think about it! Well, look at you, Alice.' Abby smirked.

'I also want to point out you managed to say at least three full sentences to Gary, and you didn't die!'

Alice gritted her teeth; now, out of pure defiance, Alice stood and headed for the water, leaving Abby with her mouth wide agape. Gary was waving at her, almost cheering her on. Alice made it to the water's edge without making a fool of herself.

Not so bad, she thought. Walking out into the water, she dove under a wave, surprising herself once again. Coming to the surface, she was pretty chuffed and turned towards Gary with a ridiculous smile on her face. Without noticing, Bobby Mullins had snuck up behind her and dived under the water; suddenly, she felt her feet go from under her, her head banging on the ocean floor, still unable to get her footing. She was tossed over and over into the shallow water, unable to find the surface; eventually, she dragged herself up, coughing and spluttering. Nearby, Bobby was in the water, laughing and pointing at her. Making sure everyone saw what had happened. Gary was making his way towards her in the water, and Abby was running down from the beach.

'Alice, are you okay?'

'I think so, I don't know, I've hit my head.' She felt woozy from swallowing so much water.

'Shut up, Bobby,' Abby yelled. 'Why are you such a jerk?'

'Come on, Alice; I'll help you up.'

Alice was mortified; she hung her head, trying to put one foot in front of the other; her head was pounding as she headed back to her towel.

Harmless, she thought, *real bloody harmless.* Bobby Mullins was an arsehole. He wasn't harmless; he could cause actual harm without thinking twice. Alice could feel the burn rising in her belly, the dark thoughts creeping forward. She went silent, sitting back on her towel. Abby was worried. She knew Alice going utterly silent on her was not a good sign.

Alice kept her nose in her book for the rest of the day, only glancing up to keep an eye on Bobby's movements. Gary had tried to coax her back into the water, and although she knew it wasn't his fault, she had completely shut down. Too busy brooding again on all the ways Bobby had ever wronged them. He was always putting people down, gloating about how amazing he was while making others feel like crap. They needed to be free of Bobby Mullins; he needed to be no more. He deserved what was coming, and Alice was just the one to dish that out. He would not win this time. He would not bully them anymore.

As the sun set, they decided it was time to start packing up. Alice had almost finished her book and was so thankful to be heading home.

She had done it, she thought, *and made it until the end of the day*. Abby had a good day, at least. It had been a long day, especially after her run-in with Bobby. Alice heard Bobby yell that he was going to the shower block. Something about needing the toilet; he was so disgusting. Looking over at Abby, Alice called out that she was heading to the ladies' toilet before they got on the train. Abby didn't look up. She was too distracted with Mark. They had been making eyes at each other all day and sitting so close Alice was surprised they hadn't melted together in the heat.

Even better, she thought, *she won't even notice I'm gone*. Alice made her way through the crowd towards the toilets. Her mind black only focused on one ending.

A big restaurant was perched above the toilet block with wide limestone staircases on either side cascading towards the beach below. Alice could hear Bobby from outside the toilet block talking rudely and loudly. He was such a pig. She waited.

The sun had sunk lower, now casting shadows along the beach. Alice tucked herself deeper into the shadows to the side of the men's shower block, no one noticing her as they passed. She heard the tap turn off; Bobby was coming; he could never shut his mouth. She could clearly hear him talking about today in the water, how he'd taken that weird girl's feet out from under her, laughing like he was some sort of hero. Her mind went darker, and her stomach was burning. Fuck you, Bobby Mullins. As quickly as he exited the shower block, Alice stepped from the shadows and, with one great heave, lunged at Bobby.

'I've been waiting for you.'

The horror on his face as he fell over and over to the beach below gave her the satisfaction she was looking for. Alice stepped back into the shadows.

Screams rang out from the stairs below as people became aware of the contorted body lying in the sand. The group rushed over to see what was going on and were shocked to see it was Bobby. His body twisted in all directions. Quietly moaning in pain. An ambulance was called as strangers performed first aid. The kids were too in shock to help. In all the chaos, Abby looked around for Alice. She saw her leaving the ladies' toilets and walking slowly over to them. Abby and the others started giving the adults around them information to contact Bobby's parents. They needed to let them know Bobby would be going by ambulance to the local hospital.

Time flashed by as the people worked on keeping Bobby alive, only for the group to be left horrified to hear that the ambulance would be too late. Bobby was gone.

With that news, the group were overcome. Abby felt like the wind had been taken from her lungs. Mark hugged her tight. What had been a lovely day had now turned into a nightmare. She didn't care much for Bobby Mullins, but no one had wished this on him. Or had they? Through her tears, she could see Alice standing away from the group.

Surely not, no way, that was not a smirk she could see on Alice's face.

Good riddance, Bobby Mullins. You will not be missed. Alice turned and went to pack her things. She had seen Abby watching her. Accidents happened all the time at the beach. It was done.

Chapter 14

Otto's expression was one of pure confusion. *Do I know this person?* He knew he had drunk a lot, but he was sure he didn't recognise the person in front of him.

'Me, you've been waiting for me?' He was utterly perplexed, looking around to see if they meant someone else. Before Otto could think to move, he was cracked over the head with a broken brick, hitting the ground with a thud. *Nope, I don't know this person.* He tried to move, but nothing was working; he felt himself being lifted. His eyes started to close, and before he knew it, darkness.

As quick as that, Alice had managed to incapacitate Otto. She made sure to hit him just in the right spot. Unable to call for help, unable to move. This was easier than expected.

She wasn't going to finish the job here; there were still too many people leaving the clubs, and she had a bigger chance of being disturbed. She would get him to a quieter part of town, away from the extra cameras.

Accidents happen, she thought; *this would look no different.* Pushing over the trolley, she heaved Otto into it, torso first and then his legs; she knew he wasn't too heavy, but dead weight was an exception, so she made a mental note to start doing more weights. Covering him in the blankets and cardboard she had gathered earlier, ensuring he was completely hidden, she made her way out of the far side of the ally, away from the kebab shop. Slow and steady, looking down. No one wanted to make eye contact with the homeless person. It was as easy as that. She was a nobody. Alice was careful just to travel far enough away from Otto's last sighting; it would look like he just wandered away and got himself into trouble, ending up down another dimly lit ally. Alcohol could really mess with one's sense of direction. Alice stopped; she made sure to look around for any cameras she had missed on her way in, but she saw none. Rummaging around in Otto's pockets, she found his phone. Using his thumb, she unlocked it. Alice sat and scrolled through his messages to and from his father. Not many over the last three months, and none instigated by his father.

Otto, Otto, Otto, you will feel this loss no more. Your father has abandoned you. That's an awful pain for a child to have to feel. Alice had felt loss before. It had almost killed her; she would not make that mistake again. Never would she allow herself to be that close to anyone ever again. When that person was taken from her, a whole other world opened for Alice; one she knew was her calling, one she knew meant turning her back on the light forever.

The Double A's had finished high school. Alice chose to head off for air hostess training, and Abby was happy with her extra hours at Supre. Alice had been wary of leaving Abby, but she seemed happy, and Alice knew

Abby would always be there when she came back. Abby wouldn't leave no matter how many times Alice asked her to. Abby and Mark had grown very close; they were even talking about marriage, and Alice couldn't think of anything worse. Mark made Abby happy in ways Alice couldn't. Alice had had to accept that. She needed to concentrate on her plan to get out of Perth. To leave the misery of her childhood there.

Alice would make sure to come back on her breaks from training to check in with Abby and her father. Each time, things felt different, and they eventually became quite distant. Alice needed Abby, and Abby swore she still needed Alice, so while that was the case, Alice would make sure to return every time. It wasn't the same, but she was still her best and only friend. Alice would always be there.

Returning towards the end of the year, Alice realised something was terribly wrong. Abby had retreated further and further into herself, like the lost little mouse on the first day they had met, flinching at every movement. Hardly making eye contact, Abby said it was nothing. On a day out shopping, Alice noticed bruising on Abby's arm. Fobbing Alice off, Abby blamed her clumsiness. From that day on, Alice never saw her in a short-sleeved blouse again. Covered head to toe even in the heat. Mark was never far from Abby, always hovering, always talking for her. This hadn't gone unnoticed by Alice. He never let her out of his sight. Time and time again, Abby assured her she was fine, and not wanting to upset her, Alice relented. She wasn't stupid. She knew what was going on, and she would keep a close eye on Abby and Mark.

Alice flew through her course and was ready for full-time in the air before she knew it.

Finally, freedom, she thought. Unique places to see would open a whole new world to her. The biggest struggle, as she knew it would be, had been customer service, but thankfully, most people on planes weren't interested in small talk. Placing their headphones on in the first five minutes of being seated was a blessing for Alice.

Her flights east would see her relocate. She was finally leaving the dullness of Perth far behind. The fast pace of Melbourne was what she needed. She could sit and people-watch for hours in the big city, no one ever paying attention to her. Just another person in the crowd, not the weird one they all pointed at in Perth. She could go anywhere and not bump into someone she knew. She would still call Abby every week, hearing her drift further and further into herself and always telling Alice not to worry.

'Hey, Abby, I miss you. I have a flight to Perth next week. I'll make sure I visit; I'll take you into Freo for dinner.'

'I can't talk long, Alice,' Abby was whispering.

'What's wrong? What is going on? Is everything okay?'

'I don't know, Alice, I don't know.' Abby was almost crying now.

Alice heard Mark yelling obscenities at Abby in the background. He was slurring and, from what it sounded like, throwing things around.

'Don't let him talk to you like that; what's going on.'

'Alice.' Abby was sobbing uncontrollably now. 'I need you.'

The phone clicked; Alice stood frozen. What was going on? She tried to call back over and over, but no one picked up. She tried calling her dad so he could go and check on Abby, but he must have already been asleep. Her decision was made: she would fly to Perth in the morning; Abby needed her. Jumping online, she made her booking for the red-eye. Hold on, Abby. I'm coming. She wouldn't take no for an answer this time. Abby was coming with her; she was getting her out of that godforsaken place.

Abby's upbringing was what kept her in Perth. Her biological mother had not had the time for her, more worried about the next drink rather than looking after her daughter. Abby had longed for her mother's love; she wanted what everyone else at school had with their families. Punishment would even be good at this point. At least, it would mean she was being acknowledged. She just wanted to be normal, to have one friend.

It was a lovely sunny morning when Abby woke up in a quiet house. That was strange. Usually, she was scared of her mum flying into an angry rage, but the sound of silence was even scarier. It was eerily quiet. Where was her mum? Even after her drunkest nights, she was always up early banging around. Abby slowly lifted her head and listened. Nothing. Getting up, she made her way down the hall. She peered into the kitchen. At six years of age, she was far more capable than most kids, more so than any six-year-old should be.

Empty. The house was completely empty. No sign her mum had been home at all that morning. This wasn't entirely unusual for her mum not to be around, but normally, it was weekends or evenings, never in the morning before school. Abby didn't panic and slowly got herself ready for school. She made her lunch with the scraps left in the fridge and made her way slowly to school. Her mind was occupied all the way there by thoughts of where her mum might be. Abby was acutely aware that if anyone knew her mum was gone, Services would need to be called. That was the worst thing that could happen. She had to stay calm for the day and hope her mum was there by the time she got home. If she wasn't, then someone would have to make the call. She was strong and brave, but being on her own was not an option. Plus, there was little to no food left in the house. Her teacher saw her walk into class looking more sombre than usual if that was even possible.

'Are you okay this morning, Abby?' her face concerned.

'She still stinks,' yelled a boy from the back of the class.

Abby kept her eyes low; she could hear the teacher speaking to the rude boy at the back of the room. Abby wouldn't even know his name; no one spoke to her, and that's how she liked it. It wouldn't make any difference; kids were cruel, and nothing could change that; she was a magnet for them.

The day dragged; Abby worried about what lay waiting for her at home. Finally, the bell rang. Gathering her things, she raced for the door. She didn't stop running until she got home. Pausing at the door, she listened, but still no sound. Opening the door, the house was still dark and lifeless. Another piece of her heart broke.

'Mum, are you home,' Abby yelled out, almost begging to hear a reply. Silence. She dropped to the floor.

'Please, Mum, please just come home.' Tears now streaming down her cheeks. Her heart was breaking.

Deep down, she knew she would not see her mother again. At six, though, it was too hard for her little heart to deal with. Dragging herself up, Abby went to the kitchen. She would wait out the night and then think about who to tell in the morning. It wouldn't make much difference. She knew whoever it was would need to make the call. Making herself something to eat for dinner was an easy choice; noodles and half a knob of polony were all that was left. A staple of any alcoholic's fridge. At least it filled the hole in her stomach, just not the hole in her heart. She was devastated.

After a restless sleep, she woke begrudgingly. No sounds all night, no Mum there in the morning. It was still silent.

Making herself some toast and vegemite, she knew what she had to do. Once again, she made her way to school, slower than yesterday but early enough so she could wait for her teacher in the car park. She needed to see her before anyone else got to school, only just holding it together.

'Abby, my goodness, you are here early.' Her teacher gathered her things and got out of the car.

Tears streamed down Abby's cheeks. She couldn't speak. Not able to hold it in any longer.

'Abby, what is wrong, sweetheart?'

'My mum is gone.'

Her teacher froze.

'How long has she been gone, Abby? I'm sure it's a misunderstanding.'

Abby was wailing now; they both knew what would happen if they had to make the call to Services. It was something neither of them wanted to happen.

'Let's get you inside first; we can think about what to do then.'

'You have to call the police.' At this moment, her teacher realised this poor child was more concerned that something had happened to her mother's welfare rather than the consequences of having to call Services, and the last time the police were called, her mother had been found unconscious in a motel. Abby's panic had set in.

'Okay, my love, we can do that.'

They walked towards the office, gripping each other's hands tight. They both knew deep down that even if her mum were found, it would be the last night Abby would sleep in her own bed. Too many failings on her mum's part. This was the last straw. Her teacher sat her at reception and went into the principal's office. When they returned, both their faces were white. Looking at the small, helpless child in front of them, they didn't know what to say. She raised her head; they could not believe the maturity this child had had to find.

'It's okay, and I know Services are coming.' Her eyes dropped straight back to the floor. 'Please don't be sad for me. Hopefully, I will find a new family.' The principal choked.

'We are here for you, Abby, we will make sure you do, remember in her own way your mother loves you.'

'I know,' Abby whispered. Her eyes were still firmly on the floor, she bawled silently, she never looked up, but they could see her body quivering.

Not thirty minutes later, Services arrived. Abby had met them all before. The lady grabbed her hand, and Abby held tight. What lay ahead for her?

Please be kind to me, she thought.

If anyone deserved it, Abby did. She deserved to be taken care of and loved unconditionally. Time would tell.

Waking five hours later, Alice saw heaps of missed calls on her phone. *Oh no, what's happened now?* Opening them up, she realised they were from her father. A feeling of dread came over her.

'Dad, what's going on? Are you okay?'

'I'm fine, Alice; I'm so sorry, it's Abby, there's been an accident.' Alice felt herself fall. She struggled to speak.

'How?'

'A car accident, Mark was driving, he's okay, but I'm sorry, Alice, Abby didn't make it.' He sighed. 'They said she didn't suffer.'

Yes, she did. Alice knew from their call last night that Abby was already suffering. Abby had been suffering for months because of that monster. Alice's stomach burned, and her mind went black.

'Alice, Alice, are you there?' The phone line was dead. Alice was gone.

Dropping to the floor, she could hardly breathe, the burning in her stomach boiling over. How could this have happened? How could she let this happen? Alice was furious, her heart broken. She knew what needed to be done.

She spent the next week preparing to head to Perth for her best friend's funeral. Her grief took over at times; this was new for Alice to feel so much, but now she was alone; her other half had been ripped from her, and her heart shattered. She spent her days keeping up to date on social media with what was being said, she needed to know every detail. It was a new way for Alice to watch without being in the same place as anyone. She didn't want to have to be around anyone who knew her. Stories of what had happened were everywhere, some not very helpful and not holding much truth, but it started to paint a better picture for Alice that something had been very, very wrong. Mark hadn't been the upstanding boyfriend he had made himself out to be. She did admit she knew this, but not to the extent of what she was reading now, stories of people seeing Abby in tears time and time again. Mark plastered at the pub most nights. His drinking had become a big problem. They had seen him be far too physical with Abby, and they didn't want to interfere. Abby assured them she was coping, but they chose to ignore it.

The night of the crash, Mark had been drinking again. Abby was called to come and collect him from the pub like she had on too many occasions. The barmen knew their number off by heart. Sometimes, Abby wished they'd call the police when he played up. Save her the pain.

Not this again, she thought. The worst part was when she got him home. She would have to occupy herself out of the way, or he would punish her. It had become awful at home; Abby didn't know how to help Mark. Nothing she did was right. Ever since losing his job, he'd lost all sense of himself. Drinking and drinking, not wanting to see the light of day. Abby was alone. He took his frustration out on her, sometimes losing his temper so severely he would physically lash out. She had managed to keep it hidden from most people, but Alice had seen it. She didn't want her to worry, always making sure to blame her clumsiness. It scared her to think what Alice might do.

Abby had dealt with an alcoholic before. That day, her mother left, she vowed never to let anyone treat her like that again. Now, here she was, alone, desperate, made to feel less than. How had she let herself get here again?

Her childhood had gone from tragic to one filled with love. Her whole world changed for the better after her principal made that call. She had gone straight to a loving home. Never worrying about food ever again. A family that cared for her, cleaned her clothes, and ensured her life was fulfilling. It took her many months to get used to the fact that she was only a child and not an adult. She had people who liked taking care of her. She was loved.

Mark loved her, but it had gone so wrong so fast. They had been inseparable, but once again, booze proved too strong. Not even love could overcome that. Desperate to make it work, desperate to not be abandoned again, she stuck it out and tried to be the compassionate partner. Never finding fault in him, only herself.

Alice told her over and over, just leave. You deserve better. Abby couldn't, and she couldn't bring herself to be alone. She hid the worst from her. Alice would not tolerate her being hurt. Alice would not let Mark touch her. What Alice might do scared her.

Alice flew out the night before Abby's funeral. Telling no one of her plans. Her father had tried contacting her all week, but she wasn't ready to talk. Alice had her mind on one thing only, and she couldn't afford to lose focus. Waking early on the day of the funeral, she had things she needed to do. She slipped quietly out of her childhood home, remembering how many times she'd done this to go and visit Abby. Rumour had it Mark had been drinking even heavier since the accident, distraught at losing Abby.

Nothing like learning from your mistakes, Alice thought. *What a jerk.* There was no sympathy from Alice. She headed out on foot towards Abby's place; the houses had yet to wake. No one would see her coming or going. She had done this walk many times over the years; she could do it with her eyes closed. Arriving at Abby's, she made her way around the back – no movement from inside the house. Everything was quiet. She stepped inside, letting herself in with the key Abby had given her all those years ago. From where she stood, she could see Mark passed out on the couch, bottles and rubbish strewn all around him. He didn't even hear her come in.

'Wake up, you wanker.'

Startled, Mark looked up to see Alice.

'What the fuck are you doing here.'

'I am here for Abby, Mark.'

'I didn't do it... I mean, it was an accident.'

'Too late, arsehole, you tortured her, my best friend.'

'Fuck off, you psycho. I always told Abby you were weird and not to talk to you any more. You always got in the way; she was mine.'

Mark took a long swig of the stale beer in front of him. *Argh, so gross.* Alice could smell the alcohol pouring out of him.

Alice couldn't listen any more, and she had nothing left to say to this piece of shit. Taking the pillow next to Mark, she moved towards him. Darkness fell over her.

'Haha, what are you going to do with that? Get out. Who do you think you are?'

Mark went to stand, suddenly realising with horror he couldn't feel his arms or legs.

'What the fuck.' Staring down at his beer, trying to work out what was going on, realisation coming too late.

Well, that worked quickly, Alice smirked. Small quantities of ketamine and beer certainly don't mix. Alice moved closer.

'This is for Abby.'

Alice forced the pillow over Mark's face. No struggling, no screaming. Mark couldn't move. He was completely immobilised. She pushed down harder and harder. It hadn't taken long for Alice to feel Mark go completely limp under her weight. She pulled the pillow away slowly, making sure there was no movement. His eyes open bloodshot, capillaries bursting. It was what he deserved. Placing the white powder on the coffee table next to the beers, careful to wipe away any evidence she was ever there. Death by misadventure, that's what they'd call it. Mark had been in a terrible way. His heart broken. It must have been a terrible accident.

Alice turned to leave and saw a photo of Abby on the cupboard. A single tear rolled down her cheek, her only genuine tear ever, saved for her best friend. Her only true friend.

Mark was noticeably absent from the funeral. Both families were running around, concerned, wondering where he was. His behaviour had been terrible for months, but even this was unlike him. Slowly but surely, word spread through the funeral crowd, another problem with social media. The police had been sent to do a welfare check; they had found Mark. Mark was dead. Alcohol and drugs were found at the scene. Nothing to see here, just a distraught boyfriend. Some were shocked, laying blame on a broken heart; others were not so surprised, and then there were those who thought good riddance. Alice was the latter. She stood in the corner silently, listening and watching, no one paying any attention to her. Just how she liked it. Slowly, the burning in her stomach subsided, the darkness slowly fading. Her friend was at peace. It was done.

Chapter 15

Alice continued to scroll through Otto's phone. A happy conversation about his upcoming travel plans and the bright future he had to look forward to. Thousands of photos with so many friends on so many different adventures. Alice stood in the dark and, for the first time since this had begun, was hit by the sudden realisation that she might have this wrong. She was never wrong, but the niggling feeling that something wasn't right was building. Was she really drawn to Otto to release him from his pain, or was it something else? Did she see herself in Otto? Had she been blind to the similarities? Both lost their mothers, well Alice getting rid of hers, but same, Same, both having strained relationships with their fathers and hardly communicating from one month to the next and both only finding family and solace in their best friends. It hit Alice like a brick. Unbelievably the man in the shopping trolley was her!

Never had the burning been about ending this; it had been drawing her to Otto because they were the same. Two souls lost. Unlike her, though Otto still had his best friends, he still had their love. Alice had lost hers and was yet to find that friendship, kinship even, ever since. Her heart had taken many months to heal after Abby left her. It was a foreign feeling to Alice; it took everything she had not to let it take over her. Alice had fought hard to keep her feelings dead.

Alice heard a moan from the trolley. Well, there goes that plan. How could she have got it so wrong? This was new to her; she had dropped the ball. Always so confident and self-assured. She was always right. Otto was not some deadbeat that had forced her hand, forced her to nearly take his life. They had just both been searching for someone to need them. Someone to make them feel whole. What was she going to do? This had not been part of the plan.

With more groaning from the cart, Alice now had to think quickly. Otto was starting to wake up. Keeping out of sight, she headed back with the trolley closer to where Otto had last been seen. Getting close, she could hear Anna calling out for her friend, frantically searching for him. Those around her were trying to get her to make sense and tried to calm her down.

'I can't find my friend; he left the club to come to get a kebab, and now he's missing.'

'Have you tried calling him? Maybe he went back inside.'

Anna took out her phone; it was ringing, but they couldn't hear anything.

'It must be on silent.' Anna was frantic now; she had only been in the toilet five minutes if that. Where the hell could he have gone? Heidi wasn't answering her phone either, probably passed out by now. Why did Anna always have to be the responsible one, always the one picking up the pieces? Otto, where the hell are you? Turning back to the club, she went to ask security if they had seen anything or if they noticed Otto go back inside. Surely, he hadn't gone back. They were all past the point of any more drinks.

With any luck, Alice could make this look like a nasty drunken accident. Otto went into the ally to wee and fell over, bumping his head. She had made sure the hit over the head would make Otto feel out of it for a while. How had she gotten here? How had it gone so wrong? The burning had drawn her to Otto, mirroring her needing and wanting. Wanting the friendships he had, needing the friendships he had found. This was very bizarre for Alice. Maybe she hadn't realised just how much she missed Abby.

Removing Otto from the trolley, Alice laid him carefully on the ground. She removed any last trace of her ever being there and crouched next to him, 'Goodbye Otto.'

She could still hear Anna calling for her friend, pleading with those around her to help. Someone in the crowd yelled for her to try his phone again.

As Alice walked out of the far side of the ally again, she heard Otto's phone ring. Anna would find him now. She quickly switched it back on before putting it back in Otto's pocket.

'Otto, Otto, where are you? What's happened?' Anna could hear his phone ringing somewhere in the ally. Racing over to Otto, she grabbed him by the shoulders.

'I have no idea; I just remember leaving the club. My head is killing me.'

'I was so worried, Otto.'

'I honestly don't know what happened.' Sitting up slowly, Otto looked around. What was he doing here? He remembered leaving the club, but that was it.

'Stuff the train, Otto. I'm getting us an Uber. You need to rest before you get on that bus.'

Oh no, Otto thought, *look at the time.* Thankfully still a couple of hours before it left. What the hell had happened? Looking down at his phone again, Otto realised it was open on the messages he'd sent to his dad. That's right. I need to send Dad a message.

'Give me a minute, Anna. I don't want to stand up too quick.'

'Are you sure you're, okay?'

'Yeah, I'm fine. I just don't know what happened.'

'I will send Dad a message before I forget. I have been putting it off all day. I don't even know what to say to him; I just want him to know I'm still alive.' For some reason, he couldn't help thinking he had just escaped a very serious situation. The hairs on the back of his neck still standing up, gave him that creepy feeling.

'It will be okay, Otto, you're doing the right thing trying to stay in touch.' Anna messaged for an Uber. She needed to get Otto home. Even if they wanted him to stay, she knew it was the best thing for him to be leaving. He needed a new challenge, a change of scenery. Plus, he didn't have the spare cash for another bus ticket. Otto looked down at his phone, sombre in his expression. He knew messaging was the right thing to do, but each time there was no reply, it broke him just that little bit more.

Hey, Dad, just keeping in touch. I'm leaving Perth in a few hours to head to Broome. I hope everything is good at home.

There, he thought, *he'd at least let him know he was still alive and on his way to his next adventure.* Otto was proud of himself, even if his father was not. Standing up, he stopped in his tracks; he saw the three dots of a reply. He didn't even know what the time was back home. He hadn't been expecting his dad to be awake, let alone reply.

Hello son. I am glad to hear your travels are going so well. I have missed you. Sorry I have been absent, but I'd like to change that if you want to keep in regular contact.

Otto couldn't believe it; his father hadn't spoken to him since he left Germany. There were many things Otto wanted to say, but at the end of the day, this was his dad. He had been let down time and time again, but when it came to it, he was his blood and if he could help heal old wounds he wanted to try. Of course, he wanted to stay in regular contact. He may not be able to forget things from the past, but he would be willing to try to work through them with his father for their future.

That sounds great, Dad. I would like that. I will get settled in Broome and give you a call.

Putting those emotions aside for now, Otto stood in stunned silence. What the hell had happened tonight? First, he'd been found knocked out in an alley, and now his father had made an attempt to reconnect with him. If only he could remember, something told him, though it may be best not to remember it all. He needed to be happy in the moment. This was another huge step forward for him. He deserved to be happy.

Alice had made her way back to her hotel using the shadows for cover. It was very quiet at her end of town, so there was no worry of bumping into anyone. Any other time, Alice would be kicking herself at what happened, but she had still been in control. It was still her decision to stop it. Her decision to let Otto experience happiness in his life. She had been able to find some happiness by moving to Melbourne. She felt like Otto could have the same. Making her way up the stairs from the back ally, she retreated to the safety of her room. That was an adventure with a very different ending than she had planned. Scoffing her burger and cheesecake that had turned up hours earlier, she thought about her own family, wondering if her mother had lived a fulfilled life after what Alice had done. Then again, it had even surprised Alice how quickly her mother had given up on them. Alice had only meant for her to back off, not leave their life altogether. Ruth Munroe took the opportunity and ran. Was she even still alive? Would her attitude towards Alice have changed over time? So many unanswered questions. Maybe one day, she would get the chance to have those questions answered. She had no regrets, though. She did what was needed. Alice had needed Abby and was not prepared to lose that at that time. Thinking about family now, she would also make sure to stay with her father on her next layover in Perth. She hadn't even told him she was there this weekend. He had been a kind father; he did his best given the circumstances.

She would need to make more of an effort. To be completely alone was something Alice didn't want to experience. It frightened her now that she was worried about this. Never would she have thought being alone was a bad thing, but now, after tonight, she wasn't so sure.

Finishing her food, Alice sighed. This was not how she had planned to end the night, but it would have to do. She had an early flight in the morning, at least she wouldn't be exhausted from disposing of a dead body.

Otto waited to board his bus at seven am sharp, knowing his bag had been stowed underneath already.

This was it, he thought. *I am off.* His head was still pounding, with no idea how it had happened – a vague recollection of a homeless man, but nothing more. Anna and Heidi stood looking significantly worse for wear. Otto couldn't work out if it was the hit to the head or alcohol that was making his head throb. He couldn't believe Anna and Heidi had been able to get up to see him off. There was a good chance they were all still drunk.

'We love you, Otto; we will see you soon. Don't have too much fun without us.'

'I love you both. It won't be long. I can't believe I'm actually going.'

They hugged for a long time until the bus driver asked Otto to get on. He waved to the girls from the window, telling himself it would not be long.

The bus pulled away, and Otto felt a tear roll down his cheek, he was off on the next adventure.

Chapter 16

Alice woke early before her flight with plenty of time to get herself ready. She needed to go for a run to decompress. Chucking on her trainers, she headed out of the hotel. It was a beautiful morning; she headed towards the Swan River, following the path along the water's edge. Perth wasn't all that bad. Especially at this time of the morning, it was amazing. Thinking through last night's events, she knew she had made a terrible mistake, but she felt it was one she needed to make. The burning was telling her something very different this time. Alice thought she needed no one after losing Abby, and now she wasn't so sure. The question was how she was going to find that someone. She wouldn't make the same mistake she had just made with Otto.

Jogging is so good for the soul. How could I have been so stupid last night? I nearly let that situation get way out of control. I know who I am, and I know what drives me. I just need to make sure I keep a level head. The urges won't stop, so I must make sure I do this fucking right and for the right reasons. At least I proved I can stop if I need to. I can't have people in this world treating me or anyone else less than; someone needs to stop them, and that is me. I'm not into the blood and gore, yet no one has pissed me off enough for me to lose all control. You never know what's building in me, I guess. God help that person who pushes me that far. Mark almost pushed me there, but it was too close to home. I needed to be smart. I needed to be invisible.

Speaking of invisible, where did that bloody note come from? No one knows me, well, not the real me. I sometimes thought Abby may have had a hunch, but she never said anything. Now I don't have Abby, I have made a mess of the Otto situation. I will have to make an effort to meet someone. No way I'm joining an online app. I'd rather shoot myself. Eric could be an option. I will have to put my feelers out and see if anything lights a spark. God, why I am still so awkward?

Shaking off her thoughts, she hoped the running would help clear her mind, not muddle it even more. It was amazing how some self-love made you feel so much better or made you think it would. Making her way back towards the hotel, she was feeling happy. She needed to get herself ready for the flight back to Melbourne. It was time to put on her work face.

Her air hostess uniform was worlds apart from the homeless look she had chosen last night. Alice could see why she often got the reaction she did from men. When she was younger, she had no idea how to use her looks to her advantage, but now she was more than aware of what she could get with them.

Making her way to the lobby, she saw Eric restocking the bar.

'See you, Eric. Hope last night wasn't too exhausting.'

'Oh, bye, Alice, can't say I'm not shattered this morning and would have preferred a lie-in, but work is work. I guess I'll see you in a couple of weeks?'

'Will do, take care. It was really nice chatting with you last night, Eric.'

Was that small talk, Alice Munroe? What is going on with you? Abby would have been all over this if she had been here. Flashing her million-dollar smile, she saw Eric pause.

Well, maybe he was interested after all. I'll have to follow up on that when I'm back, she thought. She could think of worse ways to spend her layover.

Alice stood at the counter checking in her customers. The plane was delayed, and tensions were high – just another fun day as an air hostess. A very loud, obnoxious woman could be heard towards the back of the line.

Here we go again, thought Alice, *another self-entitled middle-aged woman, more important than anyone else.* Alice had heard it all before, but this was no typical day for her.

'Can I help you?' Alice asked. Ready for whatever this woman could throw at her.

'God, are you about twelve? Don't think you can help me love.'

'Apologies, I work for the airline, and I am the person appointed to help you.' Look at her go; the customer service skills she had learnt coming into play.

'I said I'm not talking to you about anything, you little upstart, get the manager.' Marvellous, what a lovely lady. Her day had started out so well.

'Not a problem, they will be with you shortly.'

In the chaos, Alice didn't notice a woman sitting off to the side, taking in the whole scene. The woman had seen this play out before, and she had seen that look on Alice's face. She knew what was coming. It wouldn't be anything good.

As Alice turned to walk away, she heard the woman continue to abuse her. Turning, she could see the lady pointing and laughing at her. Everyone around this painful woman didn't know where to look. They were horrified but too afraid to stand up to her. She kept mocking Alice and her fellow hosties.

What a disgrace she is, thought Alice. *How dare she make this an awful flight for those around her.*

It started slow and steady. Alice could feel the burn. She could feel herself trailing off into the black. Behind her, she could still hear the woman carrying on. Alice called her manager to explain the situation. Then, her mind went dark. Alice was back.

Game on.

Chapter 17

'Woman's body found at airport car park.'

This was the headline of every newspaper front cover and TV news special on every channel. *A terrible incident has occurred at Melbourne airport's car park. A lady returning to her car has been crushed by her SUV. First reports indicate the car had been left idling while she was loading her luggage and somehow managed to roll back, knocking her onto the curb and crushing her.*

Reports from passengers have been flooding in about the woman's poor behaviour before and during the flight. This leads police to believe her erratic behaviour could possibly be to blame.

Alice turned off the TV, pleased everything had gone exactly as she thought it would. No one had seen anything, and thanks to the woman's horrendous behaviour in front of hundreds of people, it made it easy to lay the blame squarely on the victim. When the evidence was laid out this nicely, it meant less paperwork for those investigating, which in turn meant less time investigating. Win, win. Thank goodness, as Alice had been absolutely unprepared for what unfolded. She was shocked at her loss of control, but her buttons had been pushed beyond. She had frightened herself when she saw the aftermath. Her emotions had boiled over. She was still coming to terms with her decision to let Otto go. She wasn't disappointed in her decision, just disappointed she let it get so far. Her next target had just fallen in her lap, and her short fuse had got the better of her. Alice had shocked herself. Never would she have thought she could be so violent. Horrifying and intriguing all at the same time. At least Ilene wouldn't be out there squawking at anyone else from now on. She would not bully anyone ever again.

'What a horrific flight.' Ilene just wanted to get home. She was over delays and little upstart air hostesses trying to patronise her. Nothing worse than no manager in sight and everyone ignoring how bad the situation is. She had paid good money and deserved to be treated as such.

Well, if they won't speak up, Ilene was more than happy too, and she certainly wouldn't be flying Flo jet ever again. Landing in Melbourne, it had taken nearly two hours for her luggage to come out. This left her plenty of time to make a complaint. 'That will show them.' She smiled smugly, pleased with herself.

Gathering her things, she headed for the shuttle, she'd parked in car park B for the cheaper spaces but chose a disabled spot for easy access. Who was going to tell her otherwise? There was no one to stop her and her bags were very heavy.

Alice had managed to grab her hand luggage and head straight through the airport with no fuss. As she passed through baggage claims, she could still hear Ilene making a scene. Now, her luggage was taking too long to come out. 'Could she be any more miserable?' Alice cringed.

Outside, the car parks were full of people rushing to get to where they needed to be. Alice wanted to leave unseen. This could make it hard. Alice made her way to an unlit corner of the arrival's pickup. She could sit and watch the shuttle bus come and go without being seen. Ilene had been so loud that she had let the whole terminal know she needed to get on the shuttle bus to her car. Nothing good came of over-sharing information. Alice knew this better than anyone.

Alice watched Ilene approach, still muttering, and mumbling to herself. Now, she had to wait fifteen minutes for the shuttle. Alice took off at a fast pace. She needed to be ready for when the shuttle got to car park B. Hiding once again in the shadows, she waited. The bus pulled in ten minutes later. She could hear Ilene struggling with her luggage on the bus. Without even being able to see her, Alice could tell she was still carrying on.

'What a nightmare of a human,' Alice whispered to herself. It had to be done. Of course, she'd chosen a disabled bay. What a self-righteous arsehole. Alice studied her surroundings carefully. No one else got off the bus, and the car park was dead quiet.

Alice heard the boot click and headed towards the car while Ilene was occupied. Alice stood close, waiting to be seen.

'What the hell, you frightened me,' snapped Ilene.

Alice raised a finger to her lips. 'SHHHH, just try being quiet for once.' Ilene stood there, mouth agape, confused for a second before starting once again.

'Look here, you little bitch, I don't know who you – '

Alice cut her off. 'Enough.' Alice clenched her teeth. 'You are a self-righteous, snivelling Karen. You are loud, obnoxious and, worst of all, oblivious to how uncomfortable you make those around you feel.'

Ilene stood there. For the first time in a long time, her mouth was closed – the realisation of who was in front of her slowly started to materialise. Alice turned.

'That's right, you little bitch, keep walking.' Ilene couldn't help herself.

Alice stopped dead in her tracks. Ilene was busy trying to load her luggage once again. As Alice turned, she spotted the keys in the ignition. Opening the door ever so quietly and turning the key, quick as a flash, she had the handbrake off and the car in reverse. She slammed her foot on the accelerator; it was enough to send Ilene hurtling to the ground, smashing her head on the curb. Alice put the car in neutral and left the handbrake off, quietly closing the door. She had a quick look around. No one was anywhere nearby. All was quiet. She headed towards the back. Looking down, she saw it had worked better than expected. The force of the car had been enough to knock Ilene off her feet. A pool of blood had started to form under her head.

'What, nothing to say?' Alice looked her dead in the eyes. 'I don't expect you'll have much of anything to say after this.'

A small whimper escaped Ilene's mouth; she was still trying to talk. Alice couldn't believe it. In a second, her rage took over. This woman still had something to say. The burning was at boiling point. Reaching for the closest thing, Alice grabbed for the luggage. She lifted the case above her head, smashing it down hard on Ilene's face. Again and again, her anger took over, smashing Ilene's face until it no longer resembled one.

'Shut your mouth, just shut it!' A crunching sound snapped her back to reality. Shocked at her loss of control, she dropped the luggage and slumped to the floor, trying to catch her breath. What had she done? She turned her hands over back and forth, unable to believe they were capable of this. This was not her. Headlights shone into the car park as the shuttle bus returned on its next run.

'Shit, Alice, get it together, time to go.'

Alice kept low between the cars as she made her way out via the back gates. Reaching her car just in time to see flashing lights heading to car park B.

Timed that just right, she thought.

Alice was relieved to be heading home, but the niggling in her brain wouldn't stop. She had lost control, lost control to the point of nearly being caught. Still shaking from what had transpired, the adrenalin had her on autopilot. She would have to think this over. Losing control meant mistakes. Mistakes meant being caught.

Alice needed a rest. She was exhausted; it had been a huge week.

Chapter 18

Alice slept like a log after her return from Perth. It had been emotionally exhausting after the drama with Otto and then the loss of control with Ilene.

Otto, Otto, Otto, you are one lucky young man. She looked at the ceiling, time to get up. A morning run was just what she needed to clear her head. She had plenty of time before her next swing to relax and get her head around what had unfolded over the last few days; she wasn't one to dwell, but this had rattled her.

Melbourne provided the escape she needed to forget about it all; there was always something going on, lots of hustle and bustle and never-ending entertainment. Plenty of people-watching to be had, her favourite pastime.

The sun was hot as Alice ran, sweat pooling on her lower back. Her legs were long and trim and carried her effortlessly across the pavement. Gone were the days Alice wasn't prepared to be seen. It was hard not to notice her prancing along like a pony. She now knew the power her looks commanded and exactly how to use that to her advantage. No feelings meant no long-lasting relationships; she hadn't had time for that, and she wasn't ready to give her heart to someone after losing Abby. The thought scared her. Abby had been her heart and soul. There had been no room for another.

While stalking Otto, she had come to the realisation that her heart was yearning for something or someone. Maybe, just maybe, she needed that person to love again more than she wanted to admit to herself. Her thoughts flashed to Eric. More than once, she'd let her mind wander to what might be. He was kind, respectful and easy to talk to, plus he made her laugh, which gave him bonus points. He had been her only real constant for two years now, every month flying into Perth and seeing his smiling face there to greet her. She felt comfortable to be herself, not exactly her whole self, but enough.

Alice Munroe, back to reality! Pushing thoughts of Eric to the back of her mind, she remembered the bizarre note slipped under her hotel room door once again. No one knew her well enough to know of her past, none of her accidents had been found out, and she had never had to explain herself to anyone. She would be back in Perth in four days. She would call her dad and see what he was up to and suss out if anyone had been snooping around. It would be hard to get much information out of him. His health had deteriorated. Alice thought he might have onset dementia. She needed to start paying more attention and get him the care he needed. It was sad to see her father this way. It was only her and him for so many years. He was the only connection she had left at home. No Abby, no mother. He was all she had.

Moving back to Perth was not an option, she'd escaped that place years ago. There was no going back. This is why she hadn't bothered to pursue Eric earlier, although the idea of a fly in fly out relationship kind of appealed to her now.

Alice Munroe wake up, relationship? Well, this run was meant to be therapeutic, but now she was even more confused. She needed a break. So much for clearing her head.

Stopping at a café, she needed coffee.

'Morning, can I please get a flat white and a bottle of water?'

Alice found a table while the waitress went to make her coffee. Alice looked around; a middle-aged couple sat to her left, ignoring each other with faces buried in newspapers. See, relationships aren't always rainbows and unicorns. To her right, Alice saw another couple closer to her age, all loved up, completely smitten with each other. Damn it, there is no escaping this. Her thoughts kept wandering back to the same thing.

'Excuse me, are you using that chair?'

Alice didn't turn around. Her face buried in her phone.

'No, you can have it.'

'Thanks.' The woman hovered but only long enough for Alice to catch the back of her as she walked away.

She sat and drank her coffee in peace, watching the world go by. The worst part now was finding the energy to run home. Alice wouldn't make it home without going to the loo, so she headed for the toilets, trying to muster the energy to get going. A man brushed past her, apologising as he went. She noticed something under her hat when she returned to her table after her toilet stop. Getting closer, she panicked. Picking up the napkin, she saw writing.

I am watching you, and it's fascinating. It would seem blood doesn't fall far from the tree.

Alice crumpled the napkin up. 'What the fuck was going on.' She scrambled outside to get some air. The room had suddenly felt a lot smaller, like it was closing in on her.

What was this? Who was watching her? And what did that note mean? The thought of another note petrified her. She had worked hard her whole life to stay hidden, never letting anyone see the real her. Now, this person claimed to know everything about her. She spun in circles outside, trying to see if she recognised anyone around her. Alice needed to get home; she wouldn't stop until she was safely inside her building.

Peter Munroe opened his front door. He stood in complete shock, not knowing what to say.

'Hello, Peter, can I please come in?' Ruth Munroe stood in front of him. She hadn't wanted to come back, but now it was time.

Peter was a shell of his former self. She worried she had left it too late to come and see him. Would he believe her? Would he even remember who she was? Ruth had to try; a lot was at stake. Peter stepped aside, still unable to find the right words. It had been years. For so many years, he had thought he would never see her again, and now here she was.

They made their way to the lounge.

'Wow, everything's exactly the same, Peter.'

'Well, I'm not much of an interior designer, Ruth.'

'This is more awkward than I thought it would be.' Ruth still stood.

'Sorry, I'm just in shock, please take a seat.'

'Thanks, Peter.'

Ruth really didn't know where to start, all those years ago she had tried to make Peter see what was coming, but he didn't want to hear it, she wasn't sure he would even listen now, she had to try and make him. This time was different; she had intended to bring to light her worries about Alice or the proof she had of what Alice had been up to, but things had taken a turn. Ruth had hidden in the background for many years watching Alice. Following the tragic events that followed her, just like she had with Kevin. Ruth knew first hand these accidents just weren't a coincidence. Her daughter was not just that unlucky. Accidents like this just don't always happen to the one person.

'Where have you been all this time?' Peter took a seat opposite Ruth.

'I've been everywhere, Peter, but I stayed mainly in Perth. I couldn't come back to the house; I couldn't get anyone to listen. I was humiliated. I love our daughter and I was only trying my best. I had to stay away.'

'I'm sorry it came to that, Ruth; I honestly didn't expect it to go that far.' Ruth hadn't either, but there was no way she could have ever gone back. Not only had Alice embarrassed her, but she had completely manipulated the situation and caught Ruth off guard. It had broken Ruth. No matter what Alice had done, she still loved her only child dearly. She had just been trying to protect her from what she knew was coming. Ruth spent many years thinking of what she could have done differently. That was all in the past now. She had spent years getting to this point, piecing everything together, years making sure Alice didn't get out of hand, years tracking not only Alice but her brother too. It had consumed Ruth for close to fifteen years.

Thankfully, Alice hadn't been hard to keep an eye on. Her life hadn't spiralled as far as Kevin's, and she wanted to keep it like that. She hadn't forgiven Alice, but she knew it wasn't something that Alice had chosen. This illness had chosen Ruth's family, and Ruth Munroe needed to put an end to it.

Being absent had taken its toll on Ruth. She had spent many years alone. She had managed to track a behaviour pattern all over the world that she knew was Kevin. Preying on those in less fortunate countries, although most of the time, he didn't discriminate. He left a trail of dead bodies wherever he went. Five or so years after leaving the wellness centre, she had bumped into Kevin one afternoon north of Perth. Kevin had walked into a café and spotted her instantly. At first, he smiled, then the cringe and smirk appeared. Waltzing over, he knew he scared her.

'Well, hello, Ruthy, long time no see.'

Ruth stuttered, 'Hello, Kevin.'

'Well, you don't seem too excited to see me, your favourite brother, c'mon, Ruthy, you know I always looked out for you.'

'Yes, you did, Kevin.' Ruth had to play it cool; she knew what Kevin was capable of, and she certainly didn't want to be on his 'to-do' list. As far as Kevin knew, or so she thought, he was none the wiser that she knew of what he had been up to all these years.

She had managed to keep him at a distance, using her own family and being busy as an excuse to avoid family catch-ups. Now, she didn't have that excuse but hoped Kevin had no idea of the situation with her own family dynamic. It was bad enough that he knew she had a daughter; she had been fiercely protective of her family, and thankfully, Kevin had taken it at face value, just as he was so protective of Ruth for all those years.

'Where's the lovely family, Ruthy? Where have you been all these years? I've missed you.'

Ruth's skin crawled. 'Oh, you know, Kevin, busy with work and family. Alice is almost fifteen now and takes up so much time.' In her haste and fear, she had let her mouth run. Immediately, Ruth knew she had made a mistake. Kevin's eyes lit up at the mention of Alice's name. The blood drained from Ruth's face. She had protected Alice for so long that one slip might have undone everything.

'Oh, little Alice.' Kevin beamed. 'I bet she's growing up fast. They always do. Tell me, Ruthy, what is she like.'

'You know, your typical teenager; socialising, lots of friends, always something going on.'

Kevin sat staring; she wondered if he could see straight through her.

'Anyway, Kevin, I must be getting back to work.'

'Okay, Ruthy. Well, don't be a stranger, I'm sure you know where to find me. I'd love to meet Alice.'

What did he mean by that? Did he know Ruth had been keeping an eye on him? Ruth stood to leave.

'After all, no one knows me better than you.'

Keep walking, keep walking. She nearly ran to the car. She could feel his stare on the back of her neck as she went. She pulled out of the car park; she saw him exit the café, still watching. Ruth knew she would have to be extra vigilant; she could not let him infiltrate her life or let him get anywhere near Alice. This had gone to plan for the last fifteen years. She could work out where he was from, scouring news reports from all over the world. He always left a tell-tale trail of little crumbs that made it easy to track him. He couldn't know he was being watched, but at times, he made it almost too easy for her to follow him, just not easy enough that the authorities picked up on a pattern.

Recently, things had started to unravel. This is what had brought Ruth back to the family home. Two weeks earlier, she had been watching Alice. Alice had been playing a dangerous game. Stalking a male through Fremantle. Ruth had been ready to stop it. Luckily, it hadn't taken the turn it was supposed to, but it had come very close. Too close for Ruth's liking. Then, without warning, Alice had struck. Ruth had been caught off guard. A woman at the airport had pushed Alice's buttons. It had gone too far. Alice had lost control. Ruth's worst fears had been realised. She had tried to scare Alice off with a note under her hotel door, but it hadn't been enough to deter her. Then watching over her in Melbourne had brought one of Ruth's greatest fears to reality. Following Alice to a local café, she had sat mesmerised by the beautiful creature that was her daughter. In a moment of madness, Ruth had approached, asking for a spare chair, but Alice did not look up. Back at her table, the quiet moment watching her daughter was crushed. In a far corner of the café, she spotted a man, cap low, staring directly at Alice. Ruth felt terror for the first time in a long time. How could she have missed this, Kevin? It was Kevin. He sat staring straight at Alice. How was he in Australia? The last location Ruth had located him in was Mexico, well over a month ago.

Alice headed to the toilets. Kevin stood, heading straight for Alice; he brushed past her, making sure he touched her ever so slightly. Like a wolf marking his territory. As he passed her table, he dropped something just under her cap. Ruth was scared to the spot, but she needed to get to that note before Alice. Too late, Alice appeared. Kevin was long gone, but Ruth stayed. She saw the colour drain from Alice's face as she read the napkin. She could feel the panic radiating from her. Ruth's life direction would now take a dramatic turn. No longer was her mission to stop Alice. Her mission was to now keep her safe and away from Kevin. His presence was enough to send Alice spiralling to a place Ruth might not be able to bring her back from. Kevin was infatuated. She could tell from only those few minutes she sat there watching him. He needed to be stopped.

'Peter, I am here because I need your help. I need to tell you about my family. I know we had our differences when it came to Alice, but this will help explain why I was so worried about her and never wanted us to be involved with my family. Don't get me wrong, I'm still worried about Alice and her behaviour, but now I am worried about her safety too. Please just give me ten minutes to explain.'

Chapter 19

The pull for Kevin was electric. He sat so close. She had no idea he was watching her. He wanted to touch her. He needed to feel her. He wondered whether she knew about him, did she know they were destined to be together. Did she know the potential that was inside her? He was here to help and guide her to her absolute wonderful self. To make her just like him.

Ruth had kept her from him; he knew it was on purpose, and he was furious. For years, he wondered why Ruth had become such a recluse. Bumping into her that day at the café had clicked everything into place. He watched the colour drain from Ruth's face after she mentioned Alice. The realisation hit him like a locomotive. She didn't want him near her child. She wasn't avoiding Kevin. She was keeping Alice from him. This made him extremely curious. Firstly, Ruth must know about him. That was something he'd never thought about before now. However, it didn't surprise him as she knew him better than anyone. Secondly, what was it about the child Ruth didn't want him to know?

Oh, this was going to be fun, he had great plans for Alice. At the time, he thought Ruth might have been on to him, always seeming to know when he was out of the country, but now he would have to change the way he did things.

While on a trip to the UK, he had managed to find some dodgy mates who pointed him in the right direction for fake IDs. This made it less likely for him to be tracked by name. Ruth had worked it out, and he certainly didn't want the authorities making the same connections. He'd spent many years trying not to be predictable while navigating the world, landing in many different countries hoping his worst desires would not be noticed. Nobody missed those that had already been forgotten – those that had retreated to the streets, the darkest areas of the big cities. America was the easiest of all, so many had turned away their family and friends already, non-existent to most. This was how he had managed to stay off the radar for such a long time. He was never in the same place for too long, always on the move, returning to Perth only to recharge and plan his next trip.

That wasn't to say there hadn't been moments when Kevin had slipped up. Mistakes had been made. Mexico was one of his favourite haunts. An excellent place for hunting, choosing victims no one would ever miss. Unbeknown to him, he had popped up on immigration's radar one too many times, heading across borders. This had aroused suspicion.

The Aussie gringo was coming and going with no real explanation or purpose, yet always seeming to have plenty of money to throw around and entice young men and women off the streets. They followed him like a harem for weeks while he gained their trust. They were bending to his every whim, wanting to please him. He took great delight in watching them fight between themselves as to who was going to impress him the most. Kevin's every desire was catered to. They fawned over him as he splashed his money around. Then, once that trust was built, he would strike, getting bored with the dance, his urge to kill taking over. The obscener, the better. Both emotional and sexual pleasure taking over. However, he was getting too comfortable in the same place, and whispers had started to spread through the community. The gringo with the money was evil and not to be trusted. Families started to report the missing, and the police started to take notice. Kevin had always worked alone, but his desire had grown so big that he needed help disposing of the bodies. Paying street rats in drugs, he would have them cart the dismembered bodies he'd chopped up in garbage bags using an electric knife. They didn't ask questions, just the way he liked it.

The problem was that they weren't always reliable, and a discarded bag was found. The remains of a teenage girl were identified. It didn't take long for word to spread. Sending him into a panic. Kevin had packed in a hurry, crossing the border, and flying out before they had a chance to catch him. It had been far too close for his liking. He had overindulged. He would need to lay low for a while on his return Perth.

It was the boredom of laying low that led to the extra interest in Alice. While at home, it had been the perfect chance to figure out what was going on. Pulling out family photos at home and seeing Ruth, his mind went straight to Alice. She had a very limited social media presence, no huge friend group that Ruth had alluded to and no other close family other than her father. By all accounts, it looked as though Ruth was absent in Alice's life, which was very interesting. So many questions Kevin wanted answered. This was going to be fun; all work and no play had driven him mad. It was time to get back out there. Firstly, he'd have to scratch the itch that had been building. He needed to be in control once he started his quest for Alice, and in this state, it was not going to happen. She was his priority now. The hows and whys needed to be solved. If he was right about this, the end game would be magnificent.

Alice spent her next three days lying around trying to catch up on the rest she greatly needed. She also thought it was best to stay in after the incident at the café. She had been spooked and hadn't quite gathered the strength to try and find out what was going on. Alice was totally confused about who might be watching her. Other than her mother, there was no one else she could think of that would even be bothered with her. She had no other family she knew of, and her friends consisted only of her work colleagues and Eric. Alice could just about go insane, racking her brain on who it might be, but she had wanted to spend the next three days clearing her head, not muddling her thoughts more.

She needed to be fresh and ready for her shift. Otherwise, there'd be another Ilene found in a car park somewhere if she wasn't in the right frame of mind. Settling in on the couch, her thoughts turned once again to Eric. She would test the waters when she got to Perth. Maybe Eric would have some spare time to go for a drink rather than have to serve them. Alice was nervous, but if anything, the last few weeks had taught her that she was very alone, not only literally but emotionally. Her heart had been crying out for someone. It needed to be needed.

Abby had walked straight into her life when she least expected it, becoming her everything. She didn't expect it to be that easy again, but she hoped she had come far enough to hold a conversation with Eric at the very least. Alice had nothing to lose.

Alice got an early night and woke ready to head to Perth. She had spoken to her father and let him know she would catch up with him while she was there. Alice had to get to the bottom of who was watching her. Hopefully, her dad would have some answers for her. Gone were her carefree days sitting quietly in the background. Someone knew about her past, and she needed to know who before everything unravelled. It was smooth sailing in the airport, with no delays and happy customers. They were in Perth before they knew it. Alice made her way out of the departure doors and headed for the exit. She got the shock of her life to see her father there waiting for her.

'Hey, Dad, this is a surprise. I didn't even know you were still driving.'

'Some things are a necessity, Alice.'

That's weird, thought Alice, *but her father had been odd for a while now.*

'Let's get you home, Alice. We have a lot to catch up on.'

'Sure, Dad.'

She loved her father dearly but had no idea what was happening. She had told him she would come to the house, never expecting to see him at the airport.

They sat in silence until they neared home. Alice had asked her father on the phone if anything unusual had been going on as she had received some weird notes. Her father had replied that all was normal, and Alice had left it at that. Alice got a distinct feeling that all was not as normal as her father had tried to make out. Walking into the kitchen, Alice froze. Sat before her was Ruth, the mother she never had, the mother she had betrayed, the mother she had wanted to just love her unconditionally.

'What's going on?' Alice was flustered. She looked everywhere but at Ruth.

'Please sit down, love, and we will explain.' Her father pulled out a chair for her to sit on.

'Hello, Alice, I am sorry to startle you like this, but we have important things to discuss with you.'

Alice didn't know what to say. Was this going to be another intervention to try and get her help, help she never needed in the first place? For so many years, she had wondered where her mother was, and now, to be sat across from her, she didn't even know what to say. So many things had built up over the years, and now, sitting in front of Ruth, she had nothing.

'Firstly, Alice, I want you to know I'm not upset with you, but I won't lie. My heart was broken after I went away. It has taken many years for me to come to terms with what happened at Dr Mary's, but now we need to move on to deal with the problems we have now.'

'Here we go again. I am not the problem.' Alice was indignant.

'No, Alice, you are not the problem at this point, but do not get me wrong, I know who you are and what you have done.'

'It was you!' Alice blurted out. 'You have been leaving me those creepy notes and following me. See, Dad, some things never change.'

'Alice, calm down and listen to your mother.'

Alice stared at him like she had been stabbed in the heart.

'Great, she has gotten to you now too.'

'Alice,' Ruth snapped. 'Listen to me. I wrote that note in your hotel room to try and get you to stop your behaviour. I thought if you knew someone was watching you, you would stop. Obviously, I was wrong. This doesn't matter now; I have some things about my family I must tell you, and then, hopefully, it will all start to make sense. Please just listen.'

'Fine, carry on.' Alice slumped in her chair; arms crossed like a petulant teenager.

Ruth began. 'This is something I should have told you and your father years ago. Maybe we wouldn't have missed so many years together if I had. My family is very complicated. Alice, it is a large family, my brother closest to me is Kevin. He was always my fierce protector, but as he got older, I became aware that he wasn't all he seemed. His protectiveness became scary, finally manifesting in a gruesome, bloody game that he has continued for many years. He is a serial killer, Alice,' Ruth paused.

Alice didn't flinch. She was trying to catch up, also trying to work out how much Ruth knew about her.

'Do you understand what I'm saying, Alice?'

'Yes, you have a very dysfunctional family.'

'No, Alice, I am trying to point out that the affliction you have runs in my family. That affliction that drives you to do what you do without fear of consequences. Now, that affliction is what might push you to the extreme, and I needed to warn you that my brother will try and make sure that happens. He will make you his protégé and push you to do things you never dreamed yourself capable of. He is sick, a serial killer with no remorse. He has his eyes set on you, and I'm frightened.'

'How do you know he even knows who I am?' Alice straightened in her seat.

'I've been following him for years, and you, Alice. I saw him watching you in the café in Melbourne a few days ago. He is the one that left the message on the napkin.'

'Why would he even want anything to do with me? I am nothing like him.'

'Unfortunately, Alice, you are, you're old enough to hear this now, you are exactly like him.'

Alice looked at Ruth, the blood boiling inside her.

'Now love, just take a minute to think about it.' Her father moved closer. 'Your mother has told me about some incidents that all add up to you being involved. Alice, please, we just want to help you.'

Alice stood, not taking her eyes off Ruth.

'I need to get to my hotel.'

'Alice, we really need to talk. I have no doubt Kevin has already followed you here.'

'Dad, I'll call you tomorrow.'

She took the keys off the hook and walked out. Ruth and Peter sat silently.

'What if he gets to her, Peter? We could lose her forever.'

'Honestly, from what you've told me, Ruth, Alice is more than capable of looking after herself.'

Chapter 20

Kevin sat in business class watching his niece serve passengers. Her body language said it all, but she kept a smile planted firmly on her face. No small talk, just down to business. She had no clue who he was. Ruth had done well not letting her daughter know about the extended family. It wouldn't be long until she knew exactly who he was. He played it out in his mind over and over, fantasising about their first kill. They would be a team to be reckoned with. She would not be able to resist his charm. No one ever said no to him. He could sell ice to the Eskimos.

They arrived in Perth, and Kevin watched as Alice exited the plane. Surprisingly, Peter was at the airport to greet her. He kept his distance, not wanting Peter to see him.

He followed them to the family home and sat in his car, dying to know what was going on inside. Not thirty minutes later, Alice stormed out.

'Well, well, well, what's got her so worked up.'

He sat low in the driver's seat so she could not see him as she drove past, only popping back up once she had gone. Starting the car, he was ready to go, but the sight of Ruth leaving the house stopped him in his tracks.

'Ha, mystery solved.'

Nothing like an impromptu visit from a long-lost mummy bear to cause a bit of family drama.

'What are you up to, Ruth?'

He watched her get into her car and drive away. Surely, she wasn't aware of his new infatuation already. He had been planning to surprise her. He couldn't have her interfering in his grand plans. Taking off for the city, he knew precisely where to find Alice. Flo jet always sent their air hostesses to the same hotel, so it wasn't hard. Alice's car was parked on the street. Kevin found a spot and made his way into the hotel. Heading towards the bar, he needed to stay out of the way and not look like he was just loitering.

'Hey mate, what can I get you?' A very chirpy barman with the name badge Eric greeted Kevin.

'I'll just have a pint of lager, please; I'll grab a table by the window.'

'Not a problem, I'll have it over to you in a minute.'

Kevin made his way to the window and got comfortable. It could be a long wait until he saw Alice again. Luckily workers were finishing for the day, and the hotel was a good spot for an afternoon drink and people watching. The bar started to fill as Kevin ordered another drink. He had waited for an hour but was hoping to catch just one more glimpse of her before he headed for home.

Just as he finished his second drink, the lift doors opened and out walked the most fantastic creature he had ever seen. Alice was stunning. Her long black hair fell to her backside, her tight black dress leaving nothing to the imagination. Kevin was gobsmacked. He wasn't the only one. All eyes were on Alice as she sauntered towards the bar. Propping herself on a stool, her long legs looked like they never ended. Eric, the bartender, walked towards her with a massive smile across his face. He leaned in close while they chatted for longer than Kevin expected. Well, they must know each other well. He could tell by Alice's body language that she was flirting with him or at least trying to. This wasn't something Kevin had bargained for. Alice was his. Never had he contemplated she might have a love interest. He sat there brooding. He felt betrayed. This was never a good thing; Kevin was used to getting his own way, and he wouldn't have anyone interfering with that. Alice was his. This would not do.

Alice pawed at Eric as Eric lapped up the attention. This would not do at all. Kevin made a move to leave. He couldn't watch this any longer. Looking out the window, he spotted a familiar car. Was that Ruth? What was she doing here? Great, just what he didn't need was her snooping around. This all but confirmed for Kevin that she was either following him or Alice, and neither was a good thing for his plan.

Thankfully, it was dark enough now that he could sneak past Ruth to get to his car. He was furious. Not only with Alice for lowering herself to such behaviour with her little toy boy in front of everyone but also with Ruth. Blood boiling, he set off for the inner city. He still had an itch to scratch.

Alice was still upset as she headed for her hotel room. How dare her mother ambush her like that? How dare she tell her father things about her that no one else knew. Alice knew what she had done would never be accepted in everyday society. She didn't know why she had done it. Alice just did it and only ever to people who deserved it. She prided herself on doing what was needed, but now, who knew what her father thought of her? Her last and only family. Well, that wasn't true. She now had her interfering mother back after not knowing where the hell she had been all these years. Snooping obviously. Alice didn't know what to think just yet of Uncle Kevin, but one thing she knew for sure was that there was no way he was ever going to be a part of her life. Her mother thought she would be that naive to just let him manipulate her like that. Well, her mother didn't know her well at all. Alice was no pushover; she had looked after herself for a long time, and nothing got the better of her, especially after what happened to Abby.

She was too angry now to think straight; she just wanted to be destructive, and the best way she knew how to do that tonight was to get herself dressed up and head down to seduce Eric. She almost laughed out loud at the thought. Her, Alice Munroe didn't have a clue how to seduce anyone. The courage she never thought she had was brimming over. Somehow, her lousy mood had triggered her courage just enough that she was ready to see if Eric would be interested in a date. She'd bought the perfect little black dress, for the perfect opportunity, and this was it. If she couldn't win him over with her fantastic conversation, the dress sure would. She needed to let off steam, and other than murdering her mother, this was the best thing she could think of at short notice. If Eric was lucky enough, he'd be back in this room by the end of the night. Alice got ready and made her way to the elevator.

'Ready, Alice, put on that perfect smile!' She gave herself a little pep talk. The elevator doors opened, Alice took a breath, and BAM, all eyes were on her. The bar was busier than she thought it would be.

'Yikes, I didn't expect that.' Holding her head high, she pranced to the bar. Eric spotted her immediately, heading straight towards him.

'Well, look at you. Those four days went quickly. It's good to see you, Miss Munroe.' Alice swooned.

'Good to see you too, Eric. It's great to be back.'

'Anything exciting happened while you were home?'

Where would she even start? She couldn't possibly tell him any of it.

'An awkward family reunion, but other than that, all very boring.' Eric smiled.

'I doubt anything about you is boring, Alice Munroe.'

Alice reached out and touched his arm. 'Wouldn't you like to find out, Eric?' Their eyes came together, and Alice melted.

'You know, Alice, I think I would.' Eric turned to serve another customer. Alice could feel the heat building inside her. Woo, I need a drink. Eric returned with her favourite. She guzzled it down.

'Wow, thirsty, ha-ha.' Eric laughed.

'I'll have another one, please. I'm feeling adventurous.'

'Let's see what we can do about that.' Eric's smile and eyes broke her. Could this really work? Could Eric really fix her need? She glanced around the bar and towards the door. She was sure she recognised a man as he stood to leave. She knew immediately he was the guy from first class who was staring at her the whole flight, giving her a creepy feeling. Surely just a coincidence. Her mind travelled back to her mum's warning. No way that couldn't be him; no way he could have the audacity to get on her flight in plain sight and then turn up at her hotel. He had balls if that was her uncle. Alice made a mental note of what he looked like and decided there was no way she would let it ruin her night. Plus, whoever it was, he had left now.

Looking over to Eric, he gave her a wink and mouthed that he would be back to her in a second. Alice sat pondering. Was she just going to come out with it? She thought two drinks would be enough, but at this point, she felt like she was going to need ten.

'Penny for your thoughts.' Eric was back.

'Have you ever just thought that family was a bigger hassle than it's worth.'

'Surely not Alice. Everyone needs somebody, especially family.' She loved that he was so optimistic.

'Eric, I've been wanting to ask you something.'

'Sure, Munroe, go ahead.'

'Ooh, we are at nicknames now,' Alice gulped.

'Do you think you'd like to hang out after your shift or when you're free or…?'

'You can stop rambling, Alice; I've been waiting forever for you to ask.'

'Oh, thank God for that.'

'Hahahaha, am I really that scary?'

'Sorry, Eric, you know I'm not the most social person out there.'

'Alice, I would love to hang out with you after my shift. What did you have in mind?'

Alice hadn't thought that far ahead.

'Dinner?' She crossed her fingers, hoping that wasn't too lame.

'Sounds amazing.' Eric could sense her nervousness. 'Do you want another drink? I've got about another hour left of my shift.'

'Thanks, Eric. If I go back up to my room, I might not have the courage to come back down.'

Eric laughed; Alice really had no idea how gorgeous she was.

An hour passed fast as Alice took in her favourite pastime, people-watching. It took all sorts of people to make the word go around. All sorts of personalities somehow all working together as best they can, trying not to cause chaos in the world. It was fascinating to watch. Alice had no idea where to go for dinner, but the hotel restaurant was just as good as any, plus it kept them closer to her room.

Oh no, the thought nearly bought out hives in Alice. She needed to calm down. One more drink should do it. Eric handed the bar over to the night manager and headed over to Alice.

'It's weird seeing you this side of the bar,' Alice joked.

'As I said, it's about time, Munroe.' Every time he said her name like that, she wanted to take his clothes off there and then.

Eric guided her to the restaurant with his hand on her lower back. His touch caused goosebumps all over her body. She may have looked cold, but she was as warm as toast on the inside. Conversation flowed easily over dinner; Alice was surprised not only by her ability to maintain small talk but by how easy it was to talk to Eric. She had missed this. Abby had been the easiest person to talk to. Sometimes, they didn't even need to talk. They were just happy in each other's company. Right now, Alice felt the same familiar feeling she had with Abby. She dared to share more of herself.

'I had this really amazing friend called Abby. She was my everything. Her partner killed her in a car accident.'

'That's awful, Alice, I'm really sorry that happened to you. What happened to the partner?'

'He got what he deserved.' Suddenly, there was silence. Alice panicked.

'Oh, he had an accident not long after the funeral and passed away.'

'That's a sad set of circumstances.' Eric trailed off. Awkward silence followed.

'So, what do you want to do now?'

Phew, great change of subject, Eric. Alice was thankful.

'Well, we can always go up to my room.'

'Munroe, I thought you'd never ask!'

Laughing, Alice stood. That was as easy as she had hoped, but trepidation was setting in. She really liked Eric; she didn't want this to just fizzle out after one night. She hadn't felt like this about someone for a very long time and she wanted to make sure it was something that was going to last. As the elevator doors closed, Alice saw a familiar face staring straight at her from the lobby doors: Ruth. Ready for a battle no doubt, Alice tensed. To her surprise, her mother smiled, a kind, warm, comforting smile. Alice relaxed, and the doors closed. Grabbing Eric tight, she dragged him in for a kiss, slow and tender, her body pressed against his. She made her intentions very clear; she was ready. Her body was hot, ready to burst any second with pleasure as Eric's hands moved down to cup her bum. Alice let out a small groan as Eric bit down gently on her lip. Alice dragged him even closer.

'Munroe, you are amazing.'

'Eric, you have no idea.'

Chapter 21

Kevin's anger had exploded. His kill was swift and brutal, messy even, which was very unlike him. The homeless man had never seen it coming. Kevin's fury leaving him unrecognisable. His knife striking in and out, in and out until he was covered in blood. His anger at Alice manifesting in the kill. Gathering himself, he headed straight for the river. No way was he getting in his car like that. No evidence could be left in his car. That would just make it too easy. He waded in fully clothed, clawing at his clothes and skin, angry he was at this point because of his niece. Stripping down to nothing, he made his way back to his car in the warm night air. All was silent. No one had seen him come or go. It was done, and yet he still felt like his itch had not been scratched. He needed to concentrate on Alice, but if Ruth or Eric became a problem, they would have to go. His mind was made up. They, too, were dispensable.

Ruth smiled at Alice as the lift closed, noticing her demeanour relax slightly. Ruth would be there whether Alice wanted it or not. At least for tonight, she knew she was safe. Now, to head home and plan what she was going to do next. Peter had been great, listening to every word and vowing to help in any way he could. She had missed him and regretted not telling him about her family sooner in their marriage. Now, they could work together to protect their daughter. The only thing they got right in their marriage.

Ruth woke the next day to something she had been fearing for a long time. A brutal murder in the city. Although not his normal MO, she knew it was him. Nothing like this had happened in Perth for a very long time, and now, suddenly, a homeless man is stabbed to death in the dark depths of the city. Kevin was hunting at home. This meant nothing good for Alice. Ruth needed to get to her today. She knew she wouldn't be happy, but if Kevin got to her first, things were going to end very badly.

Ruth got herself ready and headed to see Peter. She would need him on her side if Alice was going to listen.

'Peter, have you seen the news,' Ruth burst through the front door.

'Surely that's nothing to worry about. He can't be here already, can he? I thought you said he was in Melbourne.'

'That's the problem. I knew where he was, but I don't know now, but what I do know is that he's coming for her.'

'Let's just not get ahead of ourselves, Ruth. Let's just take a moment and see what they find out about the murder.'

'All right, Peter, but I know it's him, we will have to get to Alice today, at least I know it's not her. I saw her heading to her room around the same time last night.'

'Thank god for that.' Peter had been up all night trying to make sense of everything Ruth had told him. Alice had been his loving daughter for so many years, and to hear how absent he had really been had hurt. Ruth had told him not to be silly; Alice was cunning, and he had no reason to suspect a thing. It still hurt. Had his daughter been suffering in silence? If only he had listened to Ruth all those years ago. Now, it was up to him to help make things right and get Alice the help she desperately needed. He had even looked to see if Dr Mary was still practising but thought best to leave it in case, he and Ruth both ended up in the wellness clinic this time.

Ruth and Peter spent the morning piecing together the news story and the possible connection to Kevin, the best Ruth had was that a knife was used – Kevin's weapon of choice.

'We can always drive past his house and see if there are any signs of him.'

'That's a good idea, Ruth. I'll get the keys.'

They headed for the north of Perth. They wanted to be a hundred per cent sure before they went to Alice. Anything else, and they could really put her offside. The drive was quiet, both weighing up the situation if Kevin was there.

'Drive past the house first, Peter, so we can see if his car is there.'

'Okay, Ruth.'

'Peter, he's there. Keep going and turn around at the end of the block.' Ruth's heart was pumping.

Peter turned around, and they parked a few houses down from Kevin's. They couldn't see any movement inside but made the decision to sit and watch for a while. Little did they know Kevin was inside, hard at work.

Alice woke from what seemed like a dream. Her night with Eric had been everything she had hoped for and more. She lay next to him, not wanting the moment to end. Eric had promised this wasn't just a fling for him either. Alice had needed this with every inch of her soul, to be needed again bought comfort.

Eric opened his eyes. Alice rolled over so she wasn't staring straight at him. She didn't want to freak him out.

'Morning, Munroe, these hotel beds are amazing.'

'You're not so bad yourself.' Alice blushed.

'Well, well, well, look at you with the compliments.' Eric laughed. 'You, Alice, are amazing. I really enjoyed last night. Do you think you're up for another catch-up after my afternoon shift?'

Alice was elated. She hadn't known how to ask the question, but of course, she wanted to see him tonight.

'Sounds great.' She leant in and kissed him.

'I have some things to do this morning and then an afternoon shift. I should be finished about five.'

'Okay, I'm not planning on doing a lot today.'

Eric kissed her nose and got up to shower. Alice didn't want to move, trying to savour every last second in her bed after last night.

As Eric came back in, Alice was finally up putting on her jogging gear.

'I'll head down with you and go for a run. It's great weather out there.'

'I really had a great time, Alice.'

Outside the hotel, they held each other for a long time, drawing close for a goodbye kiss. Eventually, they peeled away from each other, Eric heading for his car and Alice heading out on her run. Neither of them noticed the man sitting in his car watching them. If they had, they would have seen the look of complete disgust and betrayal on his face.

Kevin was livid. Eric had to go. As he sat there seething, he was thinking about creative ways he was going to make Eric disappear, and then it clicked: he would make Alice do it! This would be the way to get her completely on board. It would completely break her. Eric was closer to her than Kevin had first presumed, and he didn't need her affection for him getting in the way of his plans. Alice needed no ties if this was going to work. Starting his car, Kevin got ready to follow Eric. He would let him drive home and then start his plan. Seething as he drove, momentum building, Kevin was ready to end this and start his next chapter with Alice.

Kevin parked across the road from Eric's as Eric pulled into the drive. Unsure of how this was going to play out but all he knew was he needed to get Eric in his vehicle.

Racing over before he could get out of the car, Kevin knocked on the window.

'Hello there.' Eric was on his phone. 'Sorry to interrupt you, I think there is something wrong with my tyre, and I'm not strong enough to get it off. Can you help?' Eric hung up.

'Sure thing.' Kevin patted himself on the back. Playing the old and feeble card worked every time.

Kevin walked to the curb side of his car; Eric followed just as planned. As he bent down to check out the tyre, Kevin brought the tyre iron down hard across the back of his head, knocking him clean out as quickly as that. He had Eric bundled up in the back seat in no time, quickly tying his hands and feet with cable ties. Looking up to have a quick look around, no one was watching. He closed the door and pulled away cautiously, heading for home. Now wasn't the time to be driving erratic with an unconscious person in the back.

Ruth and Peter had been sitting outside of Kevin's for an hour or so before there was movement. Kevin came out of the house carrying a large duffle bag.

'Quick, duck down, don't let him see us.'

They stayed low until Kevin drove past. When he got around the corner out of sight, they headed towards the house. There were no lights on inside, and everything seemed in place. No signs that he had been up to anything. If only they had of been able to see in the spare room window. Eric lay tied up waiting to be rescued.

'What do you want to do now, Ruth?'

'He's up to something, Peter. We need to get to Alice.'

'Let's just pray that's not where Kevin was headed.' Peter was worried.

Chapter 22

Alice left her room around five, knowing Eric would be finishing his shift. Heading straight to the bar, she wasn't sure of their plans; she was just happy to spend time with Eric again. Alice got to the bar and couldn't see Eric anywhere, thinking maybe he was just finishing up out the back.

She took a seat and waited. The longer she was there, the more she worried she had been stood up. Where was he?

'Sorry, have you seen Eric?' she asked the other guy serving.

'Eric didn't turn up for his shift today. None of us have heard from him. He never does this, and he hasn't even bothered to call.'

Alice froze. Where was Eric? She tried calling his phone, but it went straight to voicemail.

Alice went to stand, starting to really panic. A hand grabbed her shoulder roughly. She spun around, coming face to face with Kevin.

'You!'

'Hello, Alice, we finally meet. I am your uncle, Kevin.' he smirked. 'I'm going to need you to come with me; don't make a fuss now.'

'I'm not going anywhere with you.'

'I thought you might say that. I have something to show you.'

Kevin pulled out his phone. Alice looked in horror as Eric appeared on the screen. Tied and bound, he looked in bad shape. Dried blood stuck to his hair and face.

'Now, Alice, we are going to leave here together without making a scene, and if you can behave, I'll take you to him.'

Alice's phone pinged. She could see a message from her father saying they were on their way to see her. Kevin grabbed the phone placing it on the counter. She needed to leave some sign so her father knew where she was.

'As I said, let's try again. It's nice and casual.'

Alice couldn't think fast enough. She needed to go with him to find Eric, which meant placing herself in great danger. The one thing she had promised she wouldn't do when it came to Kevin.

'Just a moment, I'll go with you. I need to pay.'

Kevin watched her like a hawk as she went to pay, leaning over the counter. She managed to lean down hard enough over her phone to trigger the emergency SOS.

Leaving with Kevin, her mind was a blur; she had thought she would be ready for anything, but now Eric was involved, all because of her and her messed up family.

She got into Kevin's car, and they pulled away.

'Where are we going?'

'Eric is waiting for us; I've made him nice and comfortable at my place.' Alice felt sick to her stomach.

'Why are you doing this? I don't even know you, and you don't know me.'

'Actually, I do know far more bout you than you realise. We seem to have a few things in common. Let's not play dumb, Alice. It's beneath you. We are exactly alike.'

Alice couldn't bring herself to say any more. She didn't want to face facts. She was not like him. Now, she had to focus. She had to be clever. Eric was counting on her. She zoned out for the rest of the drive, trying to clear he head, ready for anything. Kevin would not win, she was nothing like him.

Ruth and Peter pulled up just in time to see Kevin pull away from the curb outside the hotel. This time, someone was in the passenger seat. They raced inside the hotel, heading for the reception.

'Hello, can you please call upstairs to Alice Munroe? Her parents are here to see her.' They glanced at each other, allies at last.

The receptionist made the call while they paced in the lobby.

'Sorry, there is no answer in the room.'

Ruth and Peter looked at each other. Ruth headed for the bar where she had seen Alice the night before with the bartender.

'Excuse me. We are looking for our daughter. Have you seen her?' Ruth held up a photo on her phone. 'She was here last night talking to one of the bartenders.'

'Oh yeah, she was just here. You only just missed her. She left with some guy and forgot her phone.'

He handed it to Ruth, the emergency SOS still flashing. Ruth nearly fainted. Peter was there to catch her as her legs gave out.

'Peter, he has her.' Ruth held up Alice's phone.

'Where is he taking her, Peter? We have to find her.'

'He took off in the same direction we came from, so my money is back to his place, Ruth.'

Ruth rushed for the doors, barely able to breathe. Alice had been smart, but why would she go with him so easily, especially after everything Ruth had told her? Alice was too smart for that.

'Peter, something is very wrong. She wouldn't just go willingly with Kevin.'

'Let's just get to Kevin's and go from there. If it is too much for us, we will have to call the police. They will already be following the SOS on her phone.'

They raced to Kevin's, this time parking straight in the driveway right behind Kevin's car.

'Oh, thank god he's here.'

Sitting in the car, they couldn't see anything that looked suspicious.

'So, what do we do now?' Peter couldn't imagine them just walking up and knocking on the door, but that was precisely where Ruth was headed.

Kevin pulled into his driveway and walked Alice inside. Alice could tell Kevin was unhinged, not the cool, calculating uncle her mother had described. Something had sent him into a spiral of rage.

'Where is Eric?'

'Can we forget about Eric for five minutes? You and I were meant to be together. We need no interference, not from Eric or your meddling mother.'

'You are my uncle, and even that is a stretch. We will never be together.'

Alice regretted it almost immediately. The back of Kevin's hand came up quickly and hard, striking her across the face. Clutching her cheek, she retreated to the corner of the kitchen away from Kevin. She would need to be smarter, or this would be a very short game and one she didn't want to lose.

'Why am I here?' Alice yelled.

'Eric is a problem, Alice; you and I are going to be a team. He needs to go. This will be your first test. You will get rid of Eric.' Kevin's eyes gleamed. He was absolutely thrilled with his plan. Alice felt the bile rise in her throat. This man was sick, and if he thought Alice was ever going to hurt Eric, he had another thing coming.

Banging on the front door startled them both.

'Don't you fucking move.' Kevin pointed straight at her. Pulling a knife from his waistband, he went to the door.

'Kevin, I know you're in there.'

'Well, well, well, it's the meddling mother. Let's invite her in, shall we.'

Kevin grabbed Alice, holding the knife to her throat. He opened the door.

'Do come in, Ruthy. How lovely of you to visit.' Alice's skin crawled. She shook her head, not wanting her mother to come in. Pleading with her eyes for her to turn around, pleading for her to stay safe. Ruth stepped inside. She would not abandon her daughter again, Alice would not push her away this time.

'Sit.' Kevin kicked out a chair, and Ruth sat.

'Kevin, Alice has done nothing wrong. You do not need to do this. I'm the one who has been following you and interfering.'

'No, she hasn't, Ruthy, you are right. I could never hurt her; she is my destiny, and you kept her from me for so many years. Now, Alice, grab those cable ties and tie your mother to the chair.' He wasn't here to play games or be manipulated by Ruth.

'Kevin you were my greatest protector, the brother I loved dearly. We can fix this. We don't need to involve Alice.' Ruth was pleading now. Kevin banged down loudly on the kitchen counter.

'I said tie her up, Alice. I am in charge. Ruth shut your mouth before I shut it for you.'

Ruth nodded, and Alice did as she was told. Down the hall, they heard muffled noises. Kevin's yelling must have alerted Eric.

'Ah, my special guest must be awake.'

Alice made a move for the hallway without thinking twice, and in an instant, Kevin plunged the knife into Ruth's shoulder.

'Uh, uh, uh, not so fast, let's not make any silly decisions now.'

Ruth cried out in pain, stopping Alice in her tracks. 'Okay, okay, I'm not moving, leave her alone!'

'Good girl, now this is what is going to happen. You're going to sit here quietly, and I'm going to bring out our friend, and then you are going to have to decide very quickly who is going to live and who is going to die. The mother who abandoned you or the new love you are so desperate to impress.'

Alice said nothing. Her eyes though saying all that needed to be said to her mother. All the years she had missed out with her, and now all she could do was beg silently for her forgiveness.

'Do you understand?' Kevin slammed his hand down hard on the table again, making them both jump.

'Yes, I understand.'

Kevin walked down the hall and dragged Eric by his leg behind him. A trail of blood from his head wounds leaving a trail behind. Ruth too, was bleeding heavily at the kitchen table. She quickly realised why Alice had gone with Kevin so willingly. He had Eric. Ruth struggled as she could feel her eyes growing heavy.

Alice sat still, watching. She realised now Kevin was not going to hurt her, but he did want her to hurt the others. This gave her a huge advantage.

Eric's eyes were wide and scared. He was totally confused by the situation in front of him and the extra people in the room.

'Alice, what's going on? Are you okay?'

'Eric, I'm so sorry, I'll explain everything after we get out of here.'

Eric slumped. He had no idea what was going on, but blind Freddy could see it was nothing good. He was bleeding from his head, and his body was black and blue. How did he end up here? How was Alice involved in all of this?

Kevin began his sadistic dance, going between Ruth and Eric, weighing up the reasons why they should live or die. Trying to bait Alice and play one off against the other.

'Now think of this as our inauguration. This will mark the coming together of two amazing creatures. It will start our journey, two killers making their mark on the world.'

'Two killers?' Eric looked at Alice. Alice froze, Eric could not know of her past. She had to stop Kevin.

'Ha, ha, well, I guess you two really don't know each other as well as I thought you did.' Kevin loved the tension he was creating in the room.

'So, Alice, who's it going to be?'

Ruth spoke, 'Kevin, stop this, stop this now. This doesn't need to happen.'

'Hey, Ruthy, how about you shut your mouth.' Kevin lashed out again, stabbing Ruth in the other shoulder, causing her to cry out again.

Eric whimpered in the corner. Never in his life had he seen such things. Remarkably, yet scary as hell, Alice seemed far too calm for the situation, like she had seen this all before. It unnerved him more than anything else going on in the room. Her expression fierce, rather than horrified like it should be.

Another loud bang at the door stopped Kevin from tormenting Ruth.

'Open up, Kevin. I can hear Ruth in there.'

'Well, if it isn't Daddy dearest come to save the day, should we invite him in too, Alice?'

'Dad, run.' Alice screamed! Kevin lunged for the front door as Alice picked up the chair closest to her and brought it down hard on Kevin's back, causing him to hit the floor. As he gathered himself, he grabbed his knife, lashing out at Alice, wildly stabbing at anything close to him. Thankfully all he found was air.

Alice picked up Eric and dragged him towards the back door, all but throwing him down the steps to freedom. Her father rounded the back corner just in time to break Eric's fall. Alice looked at her Father, not saying a word, she stepped back inside and locked the door.

Turning and heading back down the hall, she stopped short. Kevin had her mother in a headlock, knife against her throat.

'You disappoint me, Alice.'

Ruth smiled at her, knowing what was coming. She mouthed the words, I love you, as the knife sliced through her throat. Alice dropped to the floor, screaming at Kevin.

'I love you too.' Her mother was slumped in her chair, bleeding out from her wounds.

'Look at that, just like what I did to her dearest daddy.'

Alice stood, boiling inside. *This ends now.*

Alice charged, catching Kevin off guard again. His arrogance making him an easy target. No one ever did anything he hadn't told them to do. Alice was different. He hadn't planned on her willpower. Her ability to not be manipulated by him. Alice was not like him, and she never would be. She slammed him into the kitchen bench.

'Fuck you, Kevin, you killed my mother.'

Kevin came up fast, punching her in the face. Alice went down hard; he came back again and again, kicking her in the ribs. Fury completely taking over.

Alice spotted the knife on the ground just within her reach. She reached out as he came down hard on her back. She heard her ribs crack. His insanity fuelling his fight.

Alice rolled over on the floor, slicing Kevin on the Achilles, dropping him onto one knee. He cried out, not in pain but in complete shock. No one got the better of him. Before he could think, Alice brought the knife up fast, striking him directly under the chin, the knife piercing upwards to his brain.

Alice rolled out of the way as Kevin came down with a thud. Alice lay there trying to catch her breath, a punctured lung not making it easy. It was done.

She could hear sirens heading their way just as her father kicked down the front door.

'Dad,' Alice managed to call out just before everything went black. She was done.

Chapter 23

Peter had found Alice bruised and battered, bleeding from her nose on the kitchen floor. The ambulance officers raced in behind Peter and went to work on Alice straight away. Peter gathered his wife in his arms, tears streaming down his cheeks. She had saved their daughter and lost her life even after everything that had happened. Even after they had given up on her all those years ago. He wondered how he would ever forgive himself. He wished they had more time together. He had loved her. He stared at his daughter. He should have listened all those years ago. Ruth hadn't been making much sense, but now it had all pieced together. He should have trusted her, and he should have stood by her side. Alice had needed them both. He hadn't seen it, and now the horror before him was all that was left. He needed to have a serious conversation with Alice once this mess was over. She needed help, and this time, no wasn't going to cut it.

Eric had already been taken by ambulance to the nearest hospital. Kevin had really done a number on him, taking three fingers, breaking his ribs, and a skull fracture. Eric would need a long time to heal, not only mentally but physically. What he had witnessed wasn't for the faint-hearted. Recovery would take time. Eric did not know what he was getting into, but Alice could not be blamed. No one had seen Kevin coming for Eric, and Alice would never have purposely put Eric in that situation. Her timing was the problem. The one time she had decided to put herself out there and a murderous animal had been stalking her. Talk about bad timing.

Alice sat up in her hospital bed, her injuries still needing a lot of time to heal, but she was alive, and Kevin was dead. That was all that mattered. He would not have stopped unless Alice put him down. He had forced her hand. No way would she allow him to control her, to make her like him. Alice was Alice. Kevin could not have her. Her mother was now gone. No longer would Alice need to wonder where she was. It surprised her how much that hurt. Suddenly, she realised that she had needed her mother so many times over the years but did not want to admit it to herself. Her mother had only wanted to save her and ultimately gave her life for her. All those years thinking she didn't love her, and she loved her the whole time, more than Alice could have imagined, even after all that had been done. It would take Alice time to process the feelings she was having. All this was very new to her. Somehow they had managed to break through, and dealing with them would take time. Alice had no idea how she was going to explain this to Eric, but as soon as she could get up, she was going to head down the hallway to see him. He hadn't asked for any of this, and somehow she needed to try and make things right. Eric was a good man, and Kevin would not take him from her, either.

Before she had time to think further, her father appeared at the door with Eric in a wheelchair.

'Hey, Munroe.'

If Alice could stand, she would have gone weak at the knees. Alice breathed a sigh of relief.

Eric looked far better than when she had seen him a few days ago.

'It's so good to see you up and about, Eric.'

'Don't get too excited, I am a mangled mess under this robe.'

'I am so sorry Eric.' Her voice trailed off. Her father broke the silence.

'Well, Eric just wanted to come and say hi and I am under strict instructions to not keep him out here long. I'm sure you will have plenty to chat about when you are both fully healed. A detective is coming to ask Eric some questions and they don't want him exhausted.'

There he was Pete Munroe saving the day again. Giving Alice a knowing look at the mention of a detective. Alice smiled and waved goodbye to Eric as her father wheeled him away.

Alice had a lot of soul searching to do before she could speak to either of them. She was acutely aware her father was holding back for now.

So many questions about her mother remained unanswered. One thing was for sure: as soon as she was well enough, she would delve into the mystery that was Ruth Munroe. She needed to know her mother and what she had been doing all these years. Hopefully it would bring some closure especially for Peter. She couldn't take back what had been done but she could at least try and learn from it.